THE VIEW *from* TAMISCHEIRA

Other Fiction by Richard Cumyn

The Limit of Delta Y over Delta X (1994)
I Am Not Most Places (1996)
Viking Brides (2001)
The Obstacle Course (2002)

THE VIEW
from
TAMISCHEIRA

RICHARD CUMYN

an imprint of
Beach Holme Publishing
Vancouver, BC

A PORCEPIC NOVELLA

Copyright © 2003 by Richard Cumyn

First Edition

All rights reserved.
No part of this book may be reproduced, stored in a retrieval system,
or transmitted in any form by any means, without the prior written permission of the
publisher or, in the case of photocopying or other reprographic
copying, a licence from Access Copyright (Canadian Copyright
Licensing Agency), Toronto, Ontario.

This book is published by Beach Holme Publishing
226–2040 West 12th Avenue, Vancouver, B.C. V6J 2G2
This is a Porcepic Novella. *www.beachholme.bc.ca*

The publisher gratefully acknowledges the financial support of the Canada Council
for the Arts and of the British Columbia Arts Council.
The publisher also acknowledges the financial assistance received from the
Government of Canada through the Book Publishing Industry Development
Program (BPIDP) for its publishing activities.

Editor: Michael Carroll
Production and Design: Jen Hamilton
Cover Art: Copyright © ALPHA PRESSE/TIMEPIX. Used with permission.
1901, government road from Tbilisi (Tiflis) in Georgia to cross
Caucasus Mountains and the only road between Europe and Asia,
from unidentified Briton's personal photo album.
Author Photograph: Wendy Snooks

Printed and bound in Canada by Marc Veilleux Imprimeur

National Library of Canada Cataloguing in Publication Data

Cumyn, Richard, 1957-
The view from Tamischeira / by Richard Cumyn.
"A porcepic novella."
ISBN 0-88878-441-4

I. Title.
PS8555.U4894V53 2003   C813'.54   C2003-910071-5
PR9199.3.C776V53 2003

For Alan and Steve

The region of the Tuat was a long, mountainous, narrow valley with a river running along it; starting from the east it made its way to the north, and then taking a circular direction it came back to the east. In the Tuat lived all manner of fearful monsters and beasts, and here was the country through which the sun passed during the twelve hours of the night; according to one view, he [the sun] traversed this region in splendour;…according to another he died and became subject to Osiris the king, god and judge of the kingdom of the departed.

—E. A. Wallis Budge, translator,
"The Principal Geographical and Mythological Places,"
in *The Egyptian Book of the Dead*

at moments like this I think of the Underworld
you seated there on your silver chair
all the walls stuffed with beards from the prophets
to keep in the sounds   all that longing
all those goodbyes beside the water

at moments like this I think of you
               walking down to Acheron
your secrets crossing over where the sign
beside the river reads *I flow with grief*.

—Don Domanski,
from "Walking Down to Acheron"

CAUCASIA TODAY

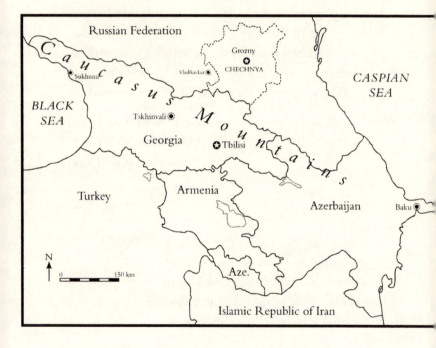

Part I

Whenever I am able to free myself from the obligations I owe my constituents, which is as often as possible without inviting censure, I travel abroad. Travel is crucial to the growth of the complete person. Vast distances and novel sensations scrape calcified deposits from the complacent ego, exposing it to the infinite strands connecting people, rocks, plants, and animal life on this shrinking orb. Invariably I return with fresh insight into particular difficulties on these honoured isles, after seeing how it is that another culture identifies and rectifies problems similar to ours.

Thus from the Chinese I learned how they could feed so many people on so little, and based on my findings while in the Orient I devised a nutritious diet of cabbage, potatoes, and whole-grain bread with added chalk as a calcium source. From a shaman of the Brazilian rainforest I learned about the extraordinary healing powers of various herbs. The aboriginal peoples of Arctic Canada are able to live comfortably in frigid temperatures in rounded shelters built wholly of ice and snow, leading me to wonder this: if such a simple material can be harnessed there, might we not have overlooked a similarly abundant resource in England to help alleviate the housing shortage in our burgeoning cities? In this regard, putting aside all thoughts of leather-lunged wolves and poorly prepared pigs, my mind lit upon the potential of straw as a building material. And yet, taking nothing from the richness, the exhilaration of these my previous excursions—across the arid Sahara, through the jungles of wildest Borneo, along the newly uncovered cobblestones of long-lost Roman towns—I can say without reservation that until my voyage to the fabled land of the Transcaucasus, I had always returned to Westminster and to my constituency office fundamentally unchanged.

My transformation was due in no small part to the majesty of the Caucasus Isthmus, a wild and beautiful girdle of land extending from the Black Sea in the west to the Caspian Sea in the east and bisected along that same axis by a range of mountains second only in grandeur to the Himalayas of Nepal. Had chance not given me the travelling companions it did, when it did, I believe I would be addressing you, Dear Reader, in a form not unlike that of my previous travel accounts. You would have open before you a reliable printed guide to one of the far-flung places of Earth, where countless strange languages survive in the hills and valleys, where blood feuds rage, sapping the populace of vitality for generations, and where hospitality afforded the stranger is unequalled. Rather, with the trip still warm and tumultuous in my mind, all my known moorings torn away as by a typhoon, I take the unprecedented liberty of exposing not only the deeds but the motivations of my companions as far as I am able to discern them. It is an incomplete, perhaps a never to be completed task. I know that I will never plumb the depths of Professor Reginald Aubrey Fessenden's extraordinary scientific mind, nor will I ever feel the intensity of the love between the poet, Archibald Lampman, whose ghostly presence I felt at all times despite the fact that I had not nor would I ever have the pleasure of his acquaintance, and Miss Katherine Waddell. Of the three, she is the one I think about most often.

The tsar had recently improved the Georgian Road connecting Europe and Asia, and it was my intention to follow it and to be open to any adventure that might befall me along its dark, winding path across the Caucasus Mountains. Although I am and will remain a pacifist, I can appreciate the effort with which Russia, having only the blunted Urals to call mountains, chose to fight so ruthlessly to secure this region. No doubt to control this most strategic and easily blocked route to the Orient, the Russians had established strict rules governing the use of the road.

When I arrived at the tariff office in Vladikavkaz that morning, they were there ahead of me, he in his mid-thirties, imposing, impatient, indignant; and she, younger, sitting as if she were going to have her photograph taken. In the little

Russian he knew, he was trying to make himself understood to the officer on duty. The tariff, as much as I could make out, was excessive. He and his companion, who was seated on a bench against the wall and looked more than mildly amused, would not pay the toll, he said. They could not do so and still afford food and accommodation along the way. The officer assumed that the woman was his wife; I could tell by the way he ignored her, an insulting failing of these outpost bureaucrats who had long ago lost their courtly St. Petersburg manners. I could also tell from the traveller's accent that he was not European, and his lack of aplomb in the situation proved that he was most definitely not British.

I did not hesitate to introduce myself and to put at their disposal the services of Sergei Borshelnikov, my guide and interpreter. Fessenden introduced himself as a professor of physics and electrical engineering at the University of Pittsburgh. Miss Waddell was from Ottawa, Dominion of Canada. The levy in dispute was four kopecks per horse per verst for the entire journey, a distance of 201 versts. We agreed to share a four-seated carriage, the cost of which worked out to be about £12, and since my publisher had allowed me that much and more for this particular expense, I offered to cover the tariff myself. Fessenden protested, although weakly. I could see that he was as tired as his companion, and that he was distracted, as if persecuted by an inner voice. The last leg of their journey, by train and steamer from Vienna to Odessa and thence to Vladikavkaz, had been a long, exhausting one with many delays.

They had found accommodation for the evening in a modest inn in town but had been kept awake most of the night by a raucous wedding celebration that seemed to involve every room but their two. I, on the other hand, had sailed from Piraeus, where I had been vacationing for a month, to Istanbul, and from there across the Black Sea to Varna, Kustendje, and Sebastopol, and thence to Novorossik, where I boarded the overnight train that runs eastward across the isthmus, arriving refreshed that morning. It was the least I could do to provide some assistance to two fellow Argonauts.

We inspected photographs of the available types of vehicle and selected a carriage that looked to be a cross between a Landau and a Brougham, with a folding top and a longer and sturdier yoke shaft than normal. It was built for four horses, with an extra horse tied on either side of the carriage, an especial arrangement meant to address the dangers of the Dariel Pass. Motor cars were not yet allowed for fear that the noise of their engines would cause rock slides and snow avalanches.

Covering our laps with thick blankets, we seated ourselves comfortably and tucked the lighter of our bags around us. The driver put the bulkier luggage into the boot at the rear of the carriage. We began with the top down. Sergei and I sat with our backs to the driver, affording the professor and Miss Waddell a view of the landscape as it unfolded. In truth, for the first part of the journey, I was content to see the vista reflected in the faces of my new acquaintances.

Reginald Fessenden and Archibald Lampman were friends at Trinity College School in Port Hope, Ontario, Canada, and they maintained a correspondence until Lampman's death in 1899. After taking a degree at the University of Toronto, Lampman taught school in Orangeville, Ontario, for two years and then accepted a position in the Post Office Department in Ottawa. Predictably he found the desk job to be dull and repetitive but not altogether taxing and a fair sight better than school teaching. Anything was better than that for a man with poetic aspirations.

The schoolroom, he wrote, placed a man exposed as a freak of culture and knowledge and longing. The little "homunculi," as he called his charges, citizens in embryo, could not for the life of them understand why they or anyone should be excited about words and numbers and ideas. He tried to infect them with his passion. He read to them from his messy notebooks and ink-smudged manuscripts all tattered at the edges and bound with string. He recited William Wordsworth, Lord Byron, Samuel Taylor Coleridge, even slipped them Walt Whitman when he was sure no one in authority was listening, and still the little savages remained impervious, ignorant of what to tell their parents about singing the body electric. Doubtless they would not have remembered the song, the singer, the point, the day, the time, the place or the weather. He felt that if he were a spring, his water might well have been pouring into a room full of sieves. Such was the character of the town, a place of stout, industrious, practical men who wanted their children to fear God, do right, accept the sanctity and redemptive quality of work, and spurn frivolity. To them a forest was uncut lumber, a stream a source of mill power, frogs overly noisy in summer, dragonflies evil-looking, and faeries not to be believed in.

For Lampman frogs were the voice boxes of the gods, while faeries pushed and pulled on every lever of wilderness. To speak and write in a way that made words dance to their own inner music was divine. And from the wellspring of idleness came peace, abiding joy, and the very reason for being alive.

In their defence, his students believed that the schoolhouse was prison, that action, regardless of how rash or ill-planned, outweighed expression, and that he was the source of their frustrations. On the same day that he caned a boy, not so much for his insolence as for his evident contempt for the contemplative life, Lampman wrote his letter of resignation to the school board.

A month later he was in Ottawa. What had his friend Duncan Campbell Scott told him about the capital city? Bundle up, even in summer, he had warned, for this was a town without time to have grown a radiant heart. They would gradually help her find her soul, but it would take some time. She needed music, theatre, poetry, and scientific enquiry. Bytown, as it was originally named, was a veritable vacuum awaiting such nourishing society as they could supply. They vowed to change that rough lumber town from one of the dark places of Earth to one of light.

I turned to the professor, remembering the location of his tenure. "Pittsburgh! Surely there is nothing in Pittsburgh but slag heaps and Vulcan stithies," I teased, trying with my quip to catch the young woman's eye. I was unsuccessful, for she sat gazing dreamily into the rugged streets of the town, her arms folded protectively across her breast.

Fessenden assured me that Pittsburgh balanced the bustle of its steel industry with a refined community of educated sophisticates who valued art, music, theatre, science, and moral enquiry. At the last item listed Miss Waddell emitted a short, explosive "Ha!" although it could just as easily have been an expression of shock or pain at the roughness of the road. She moved her body perceptibly away from her seatmate, and I wondered as to the nature of their relationship. She seemed barely able to tolerate him, but she was no captive of the journey, surely, for she held herself upright, her chin thrust forward in a resolute fashion, her eyes actively seeking the road and the passing sights. She was here of her own accord, I was certain, as much the controller of her destiny as was the esteemed inventor and teacher seated beside her.

I have, since returning from my travels in the Caucasus, read much of the poetry of Mr. Archibald Lampman, sent to me by a friend and bibliophile in Boston, Massachusetts, and have been able to compare my memory of Katherine Waddell with the poet's portrait of her in verse. An undeniable verisimilitude resides in those verses. She was tall, as tall almost as Fessenden, who stood at least six feet in height and whose girth gave him the appearance of great physical strength. And she was "slender," and "grey-eyed," carrying herself with both a "noble grace" and a "conscious dignity." All this was true of the woman with whom I came to be acquainted so intimately but who, I realise, I knew not at all. Some flame of her identity is missing, I believe, from Mr. Lampman's picture of her, although he had sought assiduously for it: "Life to her / Its sweetest and its bitterest shall reveal, / Yet leave her a secure philosopher." Close, close. The young woman I met that day in September 1902 did reveal an aspect of the philosophical in her bearing, a touch of the ascetic, perhaps, a weariness about her eyes, "mobile and deep," that came from a loss more profound than that of a few hours of sleep aboard a confined train.

Before long we had passed the outskirts of Vladikavkaz and found ourselves in the countryside following an almost imperceptible climb southward through gently undulating foothills. The road began to twist and turn now, pulling ever nearer the distant snow-covered range, while beside us the River Terek surged in a torrent. The air had a late summer tang to it of honeysuckle, dry pine, and hay.

As he published his findings in various scientific and engineering journals, Fessenden posted his friend the articles to read. In a letter dated 1893, Lampman thanks him for sending a recent article in *Scientific American*. He found it surprisingly clear. He didn't know if he would ever completely grasp Fessenden's theory concerning the transportation of sound over great distances through thin air. The poet thought himself too much a creature of his senses, confessing that what he could not see or touch he found difficult to conceive. Nature herself was supernatural enough for him. It seemed a contradictory statement, I thought, given his belief in faeries and the like.

On Fessenden's recommendation, he read *Ancient Fragments* by Professor Cory at Princeton, and another book by a man named Mead. Since their days at Trinity, they had become fascinated by a single problem, which was to locate the Pillars of Hercules marking the entrance to the waterway leading to Colchis and Eden. The textual evidence seemed to indicate that the sons of Seth had settled in Egypt or thereabouts, and at first Fessenden was convinced that the Pillars, if they still existed, would be found there. Lampman, on the other hand, doubted that Egypt was the place to search. If I have it right, he reasoned that the flooding of the Nile River, being an annual event, brought with it the fertilising silt that is such a boon to agriculture there. Josephus, he argued, described the descendants of Seth as being naturally of a good disposition, happy, remaining true to their faith, and free from evil. Like the Babylonians, they made careful studies of the heavens, and lest the knowledge of their science be lost, they recorded their discoveries on two columns or stelae, one of brick and the other of stone.

Lampman maintained they were happy because they were

far enough away from the place where the Deluge had occurred, and that the stelae they erected in Egypt must have been copies of ones lost to them after the Flood. If Josephus had meant that the original Pillars of Hercules were in Egypt, wouldn't he have said so? The poet believed that the survivors of the Flood and their descendants took with them, along with the habit of building recording columns, an abiding fear that the catastrophe would be repeated. He wrote that his "friend" at work, Miss Waddell—he had mentioned her to Fessenden in previous letters—believed that the stelae were symbols of the sexual potency that was probably universally lost for a period of time due to the psychological trauma associated with the overwhelmingly destructive force of the water. A most provocative woman.

But returning to the question, what then had the two amateur archaeologists proposed? A happy but cautious people enjoying prosperity and an expanding scientific knowledge in a new land, yet wary enough of a repetition of a cataclysmic event, something awful from the deepest recesses of memory, that they made a concerted effort to record their knowledge upon indestructible columns, one of brick which, should it be washed away, had a twin made of stone. Fair enough, but where were these monuments now? Lampman pondered. Were they under the sands of the Sahara or somewhere much farther away? Fessenden thought his friend's intuitive approach laughably unscientific, but something vague still told the poet they were looking in the wrong part of the world for the Pillars of Khur-Khal.

Out of a sense of hospitality, being the assumed host given the circumstances of our meeting, I tried to put my companions at their ease by recounting the details of a recent trip I had taken to the Punjabi region of India. Sergei, who had joined me at the Bosporus, made no pretence of hiding his boredom and promptly fell asleep. Miss Waddell appeared to warm to me or to the situation in general, and encouraged me with the occasional nod or exclamation of wonder. When I related a story of a young wife who chose to immolate herself on the funeral bier of her husband, her eyes grew wide.

"How horrible!" she cried, almost the first words she had volunteered since we had set out together, but from her tone she was anything but horrified. She shifted her weight forward, causing the fur wrap covering her upper body to slip—the air was decidedly icier now as the height of our ascent became evident—and she revealed two things immediately. The first was that she was the type of person who is fascinated by death. I can pick out such a one from a group of twenty people in a trice: he or she gazes for great lengths of time into the distance at no single point on the actual horizon, not the perfect silhouette of Mount Kasbek, say, which we were approaching, nor the sheep-dotted foothills, but longingly toward a point of inner ceasing. It is the look of one made ill by love. The second revelation was that she was holding to her bosom a square wooden box roughly the size of Fessenden's large hand, and that this item she considered as dear to her as her life. A sense of decorum prevented me from asking her directly what the box contained or why it was she guarded it so closely, and so I directed my attention instead to the professor, asking him whether he had some specific business or research that brought him so far from America.

"Where to begin. Do you know your Bible, Mr. Norman?"

I confessed to knowing only enough to get through the Anglican service without any of my constituents thinking the less of me for it.

"My father was an Anglican minister. By the time I was seven, he made sure I knew my Bible lessons better than I knew my flora and fauna. 'In the beginning was the Word.' Now I have always considered the word of God to be truth. It has to be, or where do we find ourselves? Putting the word of God on par with the word of man would make the former a variable, unreliable communication. Wouldn't you agree?"

A natural sense of diplomacy led me to nod a vigorous assent. I am not a thrice-returned Member of Parliament by mere chance. The way Miss Waddell was now contemplating her lap and sighing, however, assured me that she held a contrary opinion, and suggested that this was a discussion—an argument?—that they had had before.

"I must warn you, Mr. Norman, that the good professor likes to set intellectual traps. You have successfully avoided his first one. Similar pitfalls remain, however. For example, you are familiar, of course, with Mr. Darwin's theories contained in his *Origin of Species?*"

I was, and told her so, although I declined to admit that all I knew about Mr. Darwin's theories of evolution of life on Earth came from the synopsis my parliamentary secretary had prepared for me. Your humble representative, Dear Reader, is expected to assimilate more written matter in one session than the average person could possibly read in a lifetime.

"Then using logic and the evidence collected by your five senses—you do have all of your five senses intact, do you not, Mr. Norman?"

I assured her that I did, ceding to her sudden playfulness by asking her to call me Henry. How could someone be so distant one moment, so coy and provocative the next?

"Common sense alone would lead you to the singular conclusion that Earth and all life we see upon it today could not have been created in six days."

"Again you misunderstand what I mean by Truth," Fessenden said, no small edge of annoyance in his voice. "The ancients did not make up stories except about that which they could not have experienced. Clearly the creation of the world and the universe was something they had missed seeing by a few billion years. Their belief was in an omnipotent creator. Even today, in this new century, who of us can look about in wonder at the complexity of life and not believe in God? Dress the Deity how you will, we return always to this question of origin. I believe that we must honour the beliefs of our predecessors, and that to fail to do so is to lose touch with our origin, wherein lies our very humanity. To the ancients, a creator who could make so miraculous a planet as this must have been a being that could do it in the blink of an eye, let alone in the span of a week. I repeat my earlier assertion: the ancients held storytelling—and by that I mean fictionalizing—in low regard. Why would one make something up? Was that not lying? Look at the suspicion with which Plato regarded the artist in Greek society. Seeing the first performance of a play, his esteemed relative, Solon, collared Thespis backstage afterward and scolded him for depicting events that had not actually happened. In essence, he condemned the actor for telling lies in public."

Miss Waddell took advantage of a pause in his argument and addressed her rebuttal not to Fessenden but to me, as she might to the Speaker of the House during Question Period. "Water into wine, blind beggars given their sight, the multiplication of the loaves and fishes, the dead brought back to life—tell me these are not stories, expressions of desperate hope, even downright lies stretched into miracles by the overwrought imagination. The hysterical need to believe can be a powerful creative force, as the psychoanalysts have shown." How completely did she take us in with her false counterpoint!

"No, this are miracles, simple and plainly," said Sergei, who had roused, and who may have been playing possum all along. "Please, otherwise, where is Church? Where is faith, et cetera and et cetera?" Her puppet, her ventriloquist's dummy.

"The New Testament is practically modern history," Fessenden said, ignoring him. "By the time John dipped Jesus in the River Jordan, the imagination in human discourse was blossoming. Some of the best novels were being written by the later Greeks. What I'm trying to make you see—"

"Either we believe in Bible or we are not with God. Nothing else is possible," insisted Sergei, a quick-tongued, proud, but simplistic Georgian who was maddeningly pigheaded. I saw the divergence of their three points of view, their inability to find common ground on which to stage the discussion, to be my cue to bring it back to my original position.

"You are in the Caucasus for theological reasons then, Professor?"

"A scientific enquiry into the origins of certain recorded events. Biblical, yes, but similarly to be found in the traditions of many ancient cultures, all of which valued truth-telling above all else!"

"Point made and taken," said Katherine, about whom I was thinking in a more familiar way now ever since I had urged her to use my given name. "We'll have to start calling you Reg the Sledge!" He winced, whether under the heat of her criticism or because of the familiarity of her address—the same intimacy I now hoped for—I could not be certain.

"Archaeological in nature?" I asked.

"Yes," Fessenden said, "although I haven't the time or the money this trip to do any sort of intensive digging. Should I find what I believe is buried at various spots in this region, it would surely be the result of happy chance. No, it is simply that for years in my spare time, usually late at night after I have finished working in the lab for the day, I have been reading ancient texts and poring over a variety of maps. I reached a point at which either I would see this land with my own eyes or close the books and roll up the maps forever."

Archibald Lampman suffered from a weakened heart and lungs, the result of a childhood illness. Fessenden remained solicitous of his friend's delicate constitution throughout their correspondence. He was glad to read in a letter that Lampman had recovered his strength, and that his government job was not so odious as to distract him entirely from his writing. A foray Lampman and his literary friends proposed to take into the wilds of Algonquin Park, Fessenden wrote, filled him with no small amount of envy. At that point in his career he was one of Thomas Edison's leading chemists and would have welcomed the chance to extricate himself from the laboratory for a few days to accompany his friend on such an invigorating outing, but the work there would not wait.

They were still debating the location of the Pillars of Hercules. He thanked Lampman for his thoughts regarding Thoth, who by the poet's reckoning was the first Hermes. They were still left with the problem of geography, that is that their sources, Manetho the Sebennyte in particular, were writing in and about Egypt. By his own account, Fessenden writes, Manetho copied inscriptions engraved on columns erected by Thoth in the Seriadic Lands, which were generally agreed to be somewhere in Egypt. After the Flood, these inscriptions were transcribed from hieroglyphic characters into Greek, written down in books, and deposited by Agathodaemon, son of the second Hermes and father of Taut, in hidden chambers of the Egyptian temples. The chambers are described in Ammianus Marcellinus as "certain underground galleries and passages full of windings." This writer says that they engraved on the walls of these chambers "numerous kinds of birds and animals and countless varieties of creatures of another world." Fessenden found that last bit—creatures of another world—intriguing. Most likely, he pointed out, Marcellinus was referring to beasts of the African jungle.

He agreed with Lampman that Taautus of Egyptian and Phoenician mythology was probably the same as Taaus of the Babylonians, and that Taut and Thoth were possible derivatives of the same name. He was probably Theos of the Thracians. The name means "The One Who Does Things for the Spirits." I think of a private secretary or executive to the gods. Was he Hermes the messenger? Perhaps, thought the inventor, who wrote that he would need more evidence than they had at hand to accept that the land of the Seriad and the Pillars of Hercules were anywhere but in Egypt.

The View *from* Tamischeira

The carriage slowed almost to a halt, and the professor was interrupted by a sudden explosion of sound: deep, savage barks from an apparent pack of wild dogs, veritable wolves, that flung themselves at the auxiliary horses. Their muzzles were drawn back to expose lethal, snapping teeth, and their ears lay flat with alarm against their heads. Still more of them lay panting by the side of the road, and ahead of us blocking the way—I turned and peered around the driver's back—was a stream of sheep and goats being herded toward us in no great hurry. They stopped when they saw the carriage and parted only when they had to, when it was clear they should give way or be trampled by the shoes of our horses. The shepherds, two older men and a boy, raised their hands in greeting as we approached them but could do little to help speed our way. Their faces were sunburned the colour of darkly oiled wood, and they wore long, earth-tone mantles that covered them neck to toe, and on their heads, pie-shaped felt caps. In his hand each carried a long staff that looked to be twice his height.

"Why don't they move out of the way?" Katherine asked.

"Is no hurry," Sergei said. "Besides, is no place to go."

Indeed, close by on our left was the river, and on our right the start of a wall of rock that towered above us. The increasing roar of the Terek in its confinement was punctured at times by the shepherds calling to their flock with a piercing, high-pitched cry.

"Aleksandr Sergeyevich Pushkin travelled this way," Sergei said, "along very same road. Of course, road has been improved since then. 'We hear muffled roar and catch sight of Terek spewing forth in directions severally. Too noisy almost, the waves turning wheels of low Ossetian mills which looking like are houses for dog.' There," he said, pointing, and we saw one of the very same structures in the water. From a distance it resembled a child's miniature. "Pushkin saw Turkish prisoners—this is 1820, 1830—working on road. Being writer, greatest poet like Goethe and Shakespeare, he cannot pass by without talking to them. Like you, Mr. Norman—I am shocked you do not make interview with these shepherds for writing your book. You are quiet writer, like all English, quiet and proper. Turkish prisoners complain to him about food is given to them. All day is Russian black bread. They cannot getting used. This is making Pushkin think of friend—I cannot remember name—just returned from Paris. He is so sad. 'There is nothing to eat there,' he says. 'Nowhere could I get black bread!'"

He guffawed at his joke and slapped our knees. Finally we saw the last set of double-curled ram horns and fat, twin bustles on the hind ends of the sheep, and heard the final raucous bleat of the evil-looking, vile-smelling goats, and got our speed up once more. After a dozen versts, we arrived at a stone building that looked more like a garrison than a way station. The air felt even colder without the stream of animals to wade through, and the thought of bread made me feel suddenly famished.

Fessenden drew a long cylindrical leather case from under his seat and removed the cap from one end. From it he took a rolled map, which he began to unfurl, but because the wind was gusting crazily here and because he needed a flat surface upon which to spread it, he made quickly for the door ahead of us. So intent was he on seeing where we were in our journey that he seemed to have forgotten that a lady accompanied him. To make amends for his impetuous lack of gallantry, I went ahead to hold the door for Katherine and for Sergei who, as he drew near, feigned a blow with his fist to my midsection.

"You must upkeep your defencelessness, Mr. Norman! Is no Marquis of Roxbury rules here, I am frightened to say." And he laughed again from his belly. I did my best to ignore him.

It is not to exaggerate the point to say that Archibald Lampman shone a light upon the hitherto dim corners of his friend's mind and made him reconsider certain assumptions. As much as it pained Fessenden to admit it, Lampman may have been right about the location of the Seriadic Lands. In fact, the scientist was newly excited about the possibility of filling large gaps in the Puzzle, and all because of a shift, led by Lampman's uncanny intuition, in focus. To be precise, a shift northward. It was something Archibald had been hinting at for years, ever since he called attention to the very simple fact that although the Nile flowed from the south to the north, the ancient Egyptians grounded their entire cosmology in an east-west orientation. The mountain peak behind which the sun rose on the longest day of the year; the corresponding peak behind which it set on the shortest day; the mountain above which the sun stood at noon mid-year—where were these markers in Egypt? Or in Greece, for that matter? Or in what was then Babylon? Not there. Or, if indicated, they paled against the description of the original myth as recorded by the ancients.

He writes that he was looking at Eusebius again and was thinking about what the ancient scholar said about the Cabiri: "These things the Cabiri, the seven sons of Sydyk, and their eighth brother Esmun first of all set down in memoirs as the god Taatus commanded them." Fessenden discovered that "Sydyk" means "pointing up to the sky" and was the name given to an ithyphallic monument. The sons of Seth may well have built the stelae. Fessenden's *Stieler's Hand Atlas*, plate 49, page 19, locates a Caucasian village called Pssydache (Sydach) right in the centre of the eyot between the Terek and Sunsha Rivers in the upper Alizon Valley. This may well be the location of one or both of the lost columns.

Fessenden made another etymological point: "Seirios" until late meant the sun itself and not the star. "Seriadic," then, might mean the country of the sun (Seirios). It might mean the country of the lasso users (seira). Or it might mean the country of the Seres. The kingdom of the Seres was near the mouth of the Hypanis River, now called the Kuban. Some think the kingdom extended across the entire Caucasus Isthmus from the Black to the Caspian. This, according to a fragment of Euripides' *Phaeton*, was Asiatic Sarmatia, the land of Ur (Apollo), the place where he stabled his horses. And according to Liddell and Scott, a "seira" was a line with a noose used by the ancient Sagartians and Samaritans to entangle their enemies, and was still employed today in the region. The north Caucasus, being ruggedly mountainous, was probably not thought of as the land of the sun. Hence all the more reason for them to look south of the range.

Inside the station house we were able to procure a meal consisting of spiced sausage, kippers, and goat's milk cheese, with the ubiquitous black bread and a copious supply of vodka and wine. We helped ourselves to the buffet after Sergei spoke to the proprietor, making it clear that I would be the one paying the bill, and we sat ourselves around a plain but sturdy wooden table. Through a small window I could now see a queer grouping of animals that I had missed on arriving: of all things, a camel stood passively among a flock of chickens, ducks, and geese.

The professor had already covered the table beside us with his maps and was hunched over them, his spectacles flipped onto the top of his head and his face drawn to within a hairsbreadth of the top page.

"Reginald has a remarkable facility in one of his eyes. When he brings it close to an object, the eye takes on the power of a small microscope. I don't doubt he can see into our very souls."

The vodka had evidently liberalised Miss Waddell's manner

as well as her tongue. She seemed more relaxed and happier but was displaying also a mask of irony that I found distasteful. What circumstances had brought these two to such a level of brusque intimacy that one could be so taunting and the other so tightly closed to her provocation? They had not known each other well before coming together on this trip, of that I was almost certain, but yet they shared a distant connection. Was it a place, a person, an event? My ability to discern disharmony between two people is a skill I have honed from long hours of observation, while sharing the compartment of a train, while lounging on the deck of a steamer, and while sipping coffee in town-centre plazas the world over.

Fessenden tolerated Miss Waddell's presence, but only just. He was searching for something long-lost; a glance at his onionskin maps, overlaid one upon the other and forming semi-transparent strata several layers deep, told me so. The charts were ostensibly of this region: the boundaries of the Caucasus were there, the Black and the Caspian Seas, the mountains. But different areas were coloured variously and these had gentle, approximate curves rather than the precise, jagged edges of territory carved out by war. I made out the words *Amazon* and *Aedon*, and the top left corner of one of the pages was covered by what looked to be page references from such sources as Strabo and Herodotus.

"Although I can't for the life of me think what it is he can see on his beloved maps—he's made them all himself, you know—when he peers that closely. Fault lines? Tiny little men? Solomon's mines deep, deep under the ground? Sergei, would you be a dear and bring me another cup of this lovely turpentine?"

"Too much wodka, dear lady, is not so gentle upon stomach. I fetch you some wine instead." Sergei was as smitten with her as I was. Only the scientist appeared not to care if she was well or ill. He must hardly have tasted his food as he wolfed it down while moving his focus back and forth between the charts and a notebook he had drawn from his overcoat pocket. This, I realised, was the intense concentration, at the expense of all social niceties, that leads to great invention and discovery. This ability to block all distraction is something I confess I cannot do, for I thrive on the bombardment of stimuli from the outside world. I am a sponge for it, a dog in a field of daisies running hither and thither from bee to bird to burrow.

Sergei went to speak again to the keeper of the station, a bushy-bearded man with arching eyebrows and a full, taut belly, about tapping some of the dreadful Circassian wine that they store in sewn ox hides, entire skins minus the head, bloated with the bitterly fermented liquid. To draw a draught, one unties a cinched foreleg and the monstrous fluid gushes forth like blood. As long as he hid the nature of the wine's container from her, Sergei might have done well to woo the young colonial lass. But what was she doing here? What did she carry in that box that never left her sight? I considered warning her not to guard it so conspicuously, for then it might be made the target of one of the many thieves who populate the region.

Jewels perhaps. An heirloom. Or keepsake letters from her many admirers, love-struck Canadian cowboys and woodsmen.

In Ottawa the relentless arctic blast held the hellish frozen city in its grasp, and Lampman prayed for relief. It was so harsh, the air like ice spears piercing his lungs, that he had to swaddle his face in layers of scarves before venturing the few blocks to work. While he trudged up Metcalfe Street, he warmed himself with snatches of his favourite verse, and with thoughts of the myth lands and the possibility that they could be, of all places, in the Caucasus.

Of all the connections Fessenden had posited thus far—present-day Terek with Erech of the Gilgamesh epic, the Dariel Pass with Erebus, Sekhet-Eli with Sakatley—it was the Alizon Valley with Eden that had a lock on his imagination. To stand upon that ground, in the lee of the mountains, and to see the Garden as the ancients remembered it, to visit such a place once before death was his abiding wish. Perhaps the grip of winter had him thinking obsessively about balmy climes. But, no, it was not that alone. For all Fessenden's insistence upon reproducible, "hard" evidence, as the inventor called it, and upon logic, Lampman found himself sharing his friend's excitement for discovery, for the reality underlying the myth. As he walked home at the end of the day, or in the mornings as he ran beside the Rideau River to try to build up his wind, he would think about the journey and the itinerary when they arrived. From Sevenfold Erech of the Wide Plazas, none other than Tartarus itself with its race tracks and encircling canals, he travelled south in his mind the thirty miles to Dariel, and through it, fearful, blind in its terrible blackness, he would feel his way, the voice of the Terek his only guide until it debouched at Eshmuti, the opening to the Alizon Valley.

He had familiar landmarks in Ottawa that he associated with the Puzzle. The Byward Market east of Parliament Hill was Semochada Scheni, for it seemed that whenever he was there, surrounded by the bustle of greengrocers, butchers, poulterers, fishmongers, the crowds, the surging vitality of it, the skies were always bright. It was his Sun City, a warm oasis trapped in a heart of ice. It was Phanagoria and Phoeni and Fenkhu, all one. He wrote of a promontory overlooking the Ottawa River, which height he took to calling Bakhu, the Mountain of Sunrise, because one night he and Katherine sat there conversing until the easterly sky began to blush. The fields to the east of the city were Sek-het-sasi, for in his memory they always flamed with those first rays of the joyous day. He called a little white church where he and his love often stopped on their noontime walks, To-neter, the "Holy Land," not for its altar and hymnbooks, but for its simple pews that afforded them rest, and especially allowed them to sit close enough that they felt the conversant warmth of their bodies. For without love, he wrote, paradise is unobtainable.

Lampman was thinking as he walked alone one night, his

mind a caged rodent preventing sleep, about a riddle he and Fessenden used to wonder about in *The Egyptian Book of the Dead*. Did Reginald remember? It began, "Let me see rejoicing in these lands of the Fenkhu." The spirit of the dead is asked, "What do they give unto thee?" and it replies, "A flame of fire and a sceptre-amulet made of crystal." Lampman believed they were correct in thinking this to be a reference to a lamp with a glass chimney. The shade is then asked, "What dost thou do with them?" and it replies, "I bury them on the furrow of M'naat, as things for the night." The young men had often pondered the significance of that exchange, the burying of the lamp and the digging up of it. "What am I that am above and below?" or something to that effect—wasn't that part of the riddle? Fessenden had told him that the Caucasus is a petroleum-rich area, and that the oil is so near the surface that the rivers themselves often had a slick of oil covering them. "At the city north of the olive tree." Olive oil above and naphtha below. Would that not explain why the shade buries the lamp and then promptly digs it up, as a "thing for the night," that is, a thing that would cast a light against the darkness? The lamp, buried in loose, oil-saturated sand, would quickly fill with fuel, and the traveller making his way through Erebus would doubtless require a means of illumination, especially if Fessenden's description of the pass was accurate. The spirit sees Tartarus at a distance, makes its way through the dark defile, and comes out into the Alizon Valley at Tioneti. Knowing this, having a kind of spiritual geography to cling to, Lampman wrote that he found the dread of death to be lessened.

I left them to their various attentions: Fessenden to the reconstruction in his mind of a terrain of the imagination, a landscape I felt he knew intimately and which no longer existed as he wished it did. Hence his decision to pore over lines drawn on paper rather than direct his attention to the actual topography, a dramatic fault line cutting through massive, seemingly impenetrable mountains. This pass we were in, the Dariel, virtually the only way across—how its discovery must have seemed a miracle to the one who found it first, and how frightening the first passage must have been, through a hidden corridor that narrowed between walls so high the sun rarely touches the bottom.

Sergei I left to try his blatant charms on Miss Waddell, who appeared to enjoy his attention despite his lack of sincerity or sophistication. The smoky room and the heavy midday meal had made me slightly nauseous and so I took myself outside for some air and exercise.

I thought about what I might record in my journal that night, our destination for the end of this first day being the Dariel outpost, the true beginning of the pass that the ancients called Erebus, the "dark defile." I try with each of my books to give my readers a sense of being actually there, of smelling, hearing, tasting, touching everything I do. Already I have revealed more of the human touches than I do normally, what I shall call the comedy of the carriage, although I am not sure if everything my companions said and did can be deemed humorous. I am not even certain I will allow these observations to stand. My publisher, Mr. Heinemann, likes it so much better when I stick to the local colour. For example, like Mr. Darwin, who brought so many different species of tropical fruit and flower with him back to England, I am forever collecting specimens of plant life that I have never seen before.

As I wandered a bit away from that first station with its drab stone and its incongruous camel standing stoically amid cacophonous fowl, I saw something like a holly branch with violet berries but without the holly's protective barbs. I took also some vines of wild grape, these being fuller and of a deeper colour than those we have at home. I had brought with me a few yards each of burlap and muslin in which to wrap my findings, their roots dampened for the shipment home, the accumulated package to be contained in a porous, breathable oilskin pouch which I have found does the trick nicely through the mails. Lush ivies, their waxy leaves a blatant orange, hung crowded from a cliff above me as if they might topple any instant, and high in every recess and crevice there nestled large and outrageously flamboyant species of lichen and tripe I had never before seen, samples of which I was tempted to climb up the sheer wall to retrieve. But I was alerted—shocked would be the better word, for I had become lulled into a sort of waking dream by the dramatic marriage of massive rock and floral splendour—by Sergei's voice calling me back.

The professor believed that the Deluge was no surprise to those who had to endure it. Both Noah of the Pentateuch and Atra-Hasis of the Babylonian tradition had time to build the Ark. The Telchines had time to colonise Cos. They knew something big was coming. Both Syncellus and Eusebius, quoting from the history of Berossus, tell us that northern seals began to appear in increasing numbers as the Deluge drew near, indicating a breaking through of the Arctic Ocean into the Asiatic Mediterranean on the east coast of the Caucasus. He had seen a copy of Strabo's map showing the connection between the Arctic and the Asiatic Mediterranean but imagined that the waterway probably ceased to exist by Strabo's time. But it was there once. Fessenden believed that flooding in the far north contributed to the Deluge. He had no doubt that a study of fossils would reveal a warmer than normal spell that caused melting of the polar ice. The Flood's advance was gradual enough to allow the Cabiri to prepare.

In one version of the story, Noah or Atra-Hasis leaves the Ark in the hands of his wife and the pilot, and disappears. Those left behind thought that he had been taken into heaven, and they make no further reference to him in their tradition. But in the Babylonian story, Gilgamesh goes to see him at his old home to learn the story of the Deluge. It rather appears that he and his wife and the pilot went back home as soon as they got on dry ground. The Pentateuch says that Noah walked with God, an expression also used of Enoch. Fessenden's point was that some survivors of the Deluge did not know what became of the others, because they separated as soon as dry land appeared, and hence the different versions of the story.

Lampman suggested that he apply to the Smithsonian Institution for funds to travel to the Caucasus. He replied that although the idea was an attractive one, for the time being he was content to travel by way of book and map. Someday perhaps when his work subsided enough to allow it. It went without saying that Lampman would be his first choice of travel companion.

With fresh horses harnessed, we set off again, but with Miss Waddell and I having exchanged seats. She did not care so much to see where she was going, she said; that was outside of her control. But she would keep a weather eye on where she had been and never let it fade from her memory. I believe that is the way she expressed it.

"I have decided that each night I shall compose myself with thoughts of my imminent death," she said without warning as we accustomed ourselves to the rhythm of the road along the next leg. Her face was flushed, and she had unpinned her hair so that it fell about her face and over her shoulders in thick, sandy-coloured tresses flecked with silver and white. Sergei clucked something inane about bad luck, fumbling under the fur cloak on some bald pretence of adjusting it to bring it higher under her chin. The cad! I gave him the most disapproving stare I could muster, but he ignored me. "I would practise the remembrance of my own death," she said.

"But, dear lady, surely anything so morbid as—"

"If you would wait, Mr. Norman, for me to finish, you will see my point. Heavens, are you so quick and intrusive as this with your wife? I should say the poor woman never achieves anything resembling satisfaction."

I might have been happy to reveal my bachelorhood to her at that moment had I not felt at once chastised and scandalised by her innuendo. I would revisit this moment many months later while reading Mr. Lampman's portrait of her in verse, and wonder if he and I had met the same woman. For example, he describes her voice as one that modulates to fit each particular meaning with precisely the right chord. Her heart expressed itself transparently by way of a voice that ranged from light-hearted laughter to expressions of serious import, revealing in all a graceful nobility of spirit. I cannot deny she owned a voice that fit her visual beauty, for it was in no way girlish or slatternly. It settled pleasantly, almost musically in the middle range. If she were to be placed in a choir, she might sing alto or mezzo-soprano. True, she laughed easily, more easily after imbibing, and her laughter was as sincere as her quietest, most thoughtful utterance. In these observances the poet was accurate.

What he failed to perceive, however, and it is this I find myself returning to and dwelling upon in my analysis of the journey, is the fact of her profoundly unfettered libido, over which, as we moved deeper into the pass, like an hysterical schoolgirl taken on the Tunnel of Love ride at Brighton, she exercised a looser and looser grip. No wonder Fessenden ignored her: he was disgusted by her and wanted nothing more to do with her, and only his honour as a gentleman prevented him from shipping the woman back to the wilds of Ottawa, Canada, bound and gagged. I hesitate to publish her licentious behaviour in these pages, and only my commitment to the truth and to the ultimate benefit of mass education prevents me from exercising the strict censorship that modesty demands.

Her explanation for her decision to practise what she called a nightly memento mori was in keeping with the general unravelling of her self-control that began with the aspersion she cast upon what she would undoubtedly refer to as my "performance in bed."

She said, "I believe that we should not be ambushed by death. When it comes, it should not take one by surprise. Therefore I will embrace its inevitable approach and make it part of my nightly observance. For, after all, did we not as children kneel at our bedsides nightly, praying to God to take our souls should we die before waking?"

The professor startled us by speaking. "'But since that I must die at last, 'tis best to use myself in jest, and thus by fain'd deaths to die.'"

Not only had Fessenden been listening, but he appeared to be in agreement with Miss Waddell, who replied, "Ah, yes, John Donne, how apt. Do you find, Reginald, that when you are away from your wife for long periods of time as you are now, you 'use yourself in jest' a tad oftener than you should?" When he reddened, she turned to me. "What about you, Henry? Do you indulge in 'feigned death' whenever loneliness becomes too much to bear?"

When I protested that I did not understand what she was suggesting, she smiled wickedly at the discomfort my face betrayed. Had we been alone, I would have called her incorrigible, letting her know the extent to which I took umbrage at her suggestiveness. Perhaps this is the reason I am approaching forty years of age and remain unmarried: women are so mercurial, one minute the distant beauty, the next the mischievous daughter.

I turned my attention to the road, a welcome constant at that difficult moment. The highway was skilfully constructed, at points running dangerously close to overhanging rocks that seemed to hold their place only by the slightest of breaths. Before long we had passed the station of Lars, and seven versts farther was the gorge of Dariel, where Pliny's Caucasian Gates had once stood. The cliffs were towering parallel walls on both sides of us. Far above was a narrow cleft of grey sky. The river washed against the foot of the cliffs in places, and small rocks heaped on the roadside were evidence of the river's might. We felt no sunshine on our heads, and the air was as cold as a tomb. I can think of nothing I had ever seen before, not even the interminable sunless Arctic winter, to make me feel such apprehension, such cheerless gloom, as did this abysmal passage. The driver stooped low to lash the horses. Instinctively we grew silent, as if to speak were to call down upon our heads unimagined terrors of the underworld. Indeed, we seemed to be speeding along the very bottom of the world, and did so for a long, uneasy while until Fessenden spoke.

"'Thus far and no farther.' That is what these mountains said to Rome itself. Are you aware, Mr. Norman, that you are following the very route taken by the soul as it makes its journey through the underworld to the Elysian Fields? The Greeks weren't thinking of a place under the ground or in the clouds or on the other side of some fog-shrouded barrier. They had in mind this place here on Earth. They, the Babylonians, the Egyptians, the Semites, all, before the great dispersion of the races. Before the Deluge. *The Egyptian Book of the Dead* is, in part, a travel guide, and not to any mythical paradise but to a valley on the other side of this range of mountains. It is Eden I seek, and I mean to gaze upon it."

Unlike the three of us, who had let the gloom of the pass weigh upon us, Fessenden had come to life. Here, finally, his countenance and words revealed that he had found the convergence of his historical and geographical speculation and the terrain itself.

"But what supports your theory?" I asked him. "I am not aware of any archaeological digging taking place hereabouts."

"Reginald is not the kind of man who admits impediment,"

Katherine said.

He replied, considering her the way he might stare down an impertinent undergraduate sitting in the front row of his lecture, "The textual evidence is overwhelmingly convincing. I have no doubt that a great civilisation predating the earliest for which we have material evidence reached its zenith here, between the Black and a huge inland sea that I believe was what the ancients were thinking of when they referred in their writing to the Atlantic Ocean."

The road took a sharp turn over a narrow bridge and the gorge opened into a flat valley that spread before us. Sergei diffused the palpable tension between Fessenden and Miss Waddell—was it a question of belief or was it that every word he said provoked her?—by exclaiming that this was the same bridge Pushkin had described in his account.

"'Not far from post is little bridge throwing up across river.' When Pushkin is standing upon it, is making him think he is inside factory, whole bridge is shaking and river rumbling like wheels that turn millstones. And there," he exclaimed like an excited schoolboy, "is castle of Tamara!"

My eye was caught first by the Dariel post ahead of us, a square, formidable fortress. At each of its four corners stood a watchtower connected by high walls into which narrow slots had been cut to allow for rifle fire from within.

"Why, it's out of a fairy tale," Katherine said. "It's what we used to build out of bits of old brick and stone when we'd play knights and dragons."

"And which were you?" Fessenden asked.

We drew up to the sentry gate where a soldier was lounging before the entrance on a wooden bench. He had found a tentative spot of sunlight and was bathing in it like a cat. He stood and looked at us forbiddingly until Sergei introduced us and presented our documentation. High on the summit of a peak above this modern fortress we could see what Sergei had glimpsed earlier: the ruin of a greater, ancient castle. I took this opportunity to assemble my camera to capture a portrait of this dramatic architectural juxtaposition.

Sergei joined me, making himself a nuisance trying to help me extend the legs of the instrument's tripod. "Was impregnable home of the gorgeously beautiful and stunning Princess Tamara. Is said if her suitors could find way into castle, they were free to wooing her, but when she grows tired of them—*zup!*—she tells her guards to throw them over wall into river!"

He reminded me that Mikhail Lermontov's "Demon" was set in this same fortress.

Witness, thou star of midnight, witness, sun,
Rising and setting, king upon his throne,
No Shah of golden Persia e'er did kiss
A face so bright, so beautiful as this;
No houri in the noontide heat did lave
A form so perfect in the fountain's wave,
And no lover's hand, since Eden's days, I trow,
E'er smoothed the wrinkles from so fair a brow.

Not until I had read these lines much later, after I returned home, did I wonder if the Canadian poet, Mr. Lampman, lover of the enigmatic Katherine Waddell, had read Lermontov himself. "Houri in the noontide heat" indeed.

By the close of day we had arrived at the station house named after Mount Kasbek which, although some two thousand feet lower in elevation than Elbruz with its divided peak, is the more beautiful. Its vertiginous slopes are the steeper of the two, culminating in a jagged fist of rock thrust into the heavens. Kasbek is the sort of mountain that children draw in their school scribblers. It is Fuji-like, blue and white, conically symmetrical, with ten thousand feet of its elevation visible at a distance. It is a peak for the romantic, the solitary, the one who yearns restlessly for union but who turns away from it time and again.

The station house was a white building as raw-looking as the crags of rock surrounding us. Our horses were taken to stables that surrounded an adjacent courtyard on three sides. In the middle of the yard behind the building was the same camel I had seen back at the Balta station. He ambled over to a horse that was drinking at a water trough, and thrust his long, hairy face at the panting, slathered animal.

I could not remember our having been passed on the road by the strange animal and yet, now that I pondered it, he had been at each station before us. I asked Sergei to enquire about it.

"Is not necessary, Honourable Mumbler."

"And why, pray tell, would it not be necessary for you to

carry out my request?"

"Let me be Sherlock Holmes to your elementary Watson in this mystery. Is because you have only to employ your noodle, as it were, and answer is clarity."

"My what?"

"Noggin, thinking organ, empty jug sitting between handles of ears! Are all English so thick like potato?"

He turned and walked back around to the front of the building, and I decided then that he was nothing but an insubordinate boor, barely competent, and that I would release him from my employ as soon as a suitable replacement could be found.

Our supper that night was a buffet of *shaslik-kebab*, morsels of mutton cooked on a skewer over a wood fire. We were also served a *zakushka* of pickled fish with blackened round loaves of bread and great quantities of local wine which, if I did not think about its storage container, I found palatable. The barely cooked mutton looked to have been torn from the bone by the teeth of a wildcat. Smothering it was a tepid clot of stringy onion. In all I could stomach only a small portion. Miss Waddell also avoided the meat, choosing like me to fill up on bread. Fessenden, on the other hand, cleaned his plate of every morsel. Sergei had enticed the station master's wife to come out to the table—"This is most delicious. You are exquisite cook. Not cook? You should be!" I imagined him saying to her—and although she declined his invitation to eat with us she did treat us to a Georgian song and a folk dance, accompanied by her husband on the *balalaika*. A group of three merchants on their way to Tiflis left their table and introduced themselves and Sergei announced them. When they discovered we were English, and that the beautiful young woman in our company was unmarried, they insisted we join them in a toast. Sergei accepted and one of them handed him a ram's horn filled with wine. *"Do dna! Do dna!"* they chanted. "To the bottom! To the bottom!"

"Idiots! What shall I drink to?"

"Of course! How could we be so thoughtless? To Tsar Nicholas, the father of our feast!"

At this Sergei let a look of distaste occupy his face, but the prospect of the horn's contents quickly changed that back to his imbecile's grin, and the chant of *"Do dna! Do dna!"* resumed. The horn was the perfect design for such an exercise in excess as this, for it could not be put down on the table without its contents spilling out. To pass the horn off to someone else before it was thoroughly drained was an insult to the procurer.

"To world peace!" came the next toast after we had all, including Katherine, had a dizzying draught. She would not let us think of her as being a retiring flower. Her capacity for the bitter libation was, in fact, prodigious. When I hesitated with the bottomless horn, they cried, "What? You don't believe in world peace? *Do dna!*" The professor swallowed each draught as if it were water, letting nothing change his rather haughty, deadpan expression except for a rising flush making its way up from his neck. We toasted our mothers, true love, the mountains, sheep, Shamyl the rebel, honour, and many other things, ideals, and people I cannot remember. Everyone drank—the station master, his wife, our driver—and the horn was never once laid upon the table. An entire ox skin must have been drained.

The toasting gave way to more songs and dancing. We were all urged to stand and lock arms and circle the table. Faces flashed in a blur with one face, Katherine's, stationary before me, the rest of the room a kaleidoscope. I know that I spoke at length about the need for more modern British warships, and about the tendency of the leaves of the coleus plant to darken in direct sunshine, and about what I thought were the lessons learned in the Crimea. Why I broke my long-standing habit of moderation in drink, I cannot say for certain. It is something I regret mildly, although I am not sure I would do differently if presented with the same situation again. You might read into this a certain persuasive influence acting upon me by the group. I was away from familiar surroundings, released from the tedium of the day's travel, urged on by an insistent hospitality and the face of a woman who had already elicited in me the most divergent of responses: interest, infatuation, protectiveness, alarm, and even shame. Her look of intrigue and mischief, those slightly hooded grey eyes daring me to act outside of the bounds of the familiar, the acceptable, the decorous. She appeared to know the workings of my mind without even hearing me speak. Or did I only wish she knew? I cannot say, for then, as even now, my feelings were as new and as sharp to me as were the sight of the mountains and the bite of the cold, thin air, and the twisting passage of the road taking us from one world to the next.

I do not remember falling asleep. When I awoke, I was in a darkened room. As my eyes adjusted to the light, I saw that it was a large, open, barracks-style dormitory with ten or twelve simple beds arranged in two rows. I was still in my clothes, a single woollen blanket covering me. My mouth seemed to be lined with felt. I tried to swallow, knew that I would need to drink water soon or die, tried to raise my head, and discovered that my brain had become a heavy steel ball that jarred painfully, at the slightest movement, against the inside of my skull.

Beside me in the next bed to my left, Fessenden lay on his back, his mouth open wide like a bowl, his snores prodigiously loud. It must have been this sound that had awakened me, for uninterrupted I would have chosen to sleep until death by dehydration put a merciful end to the demonic rolling ball.

The only other occupied bed in the room was filled by the sleeping bulk of the station master who, we would learn, had been persuaded to give up his side of the marital bed to Miss Waddell, the dorm being wholly unsatisfactory to her needs. Sergei was nowhere to be seen, not that I felt any urge to search for him. Only one force compelled me up and out of the hard bed on which I lay suffering, and that was a sudden and intense sensation of *shaslik* reanimated in my stomach and bleating at me from a pit of gastrointestinal misery. I stumbled to a door leading outside and made it into the horse paddock before supper abandoned me in the most violent, inelegant of manners. Even the camel, roused from where it lay with its forelegs tucked under itself, joker and mysterious will-o'-the-wisp that it appeared to be, was alarmed. He let me cup a handful of water to drink from his trough before rising to his feet and assuming the attitude of attack. I barely had time to rinse the fuzz from my mouth before retreating in haste.

Prostrate once more, defeating another wave of nausea by an act of will alone, I felt in my waistcoat pocket for my watch, but it was not there. I have been robbed before, and have come to see in such violations the unfortunate but inevitable consequence of travel, particularly travel by the relatively well off in countries poorer than their own. For that reason I carry no jewellery but only the most utilitarian of possessions. The watch, a dependable Swiss make in a stainless-steel case, had kept time remarkably well through three previous journeys. My displeasure had more to do with my being unable to know the time—a faint grey light suggested dawn approaching—than with my having been robbed while unconscious.

"I'd say it's roughly 5:00 a.m. I don't bother with watches and clocks myself unless I have to, to catch a train, say, or give a talk." The professor's voice was low and calm, and instead of surprising me, it was soothing, as if it came from an integral part of the night or from inside me. "I believe our bodies are sensitive timepieces that know when it's time to eat, sleep, wake, work, exercise. You refer too much to an instrument calibrated to an artificial measurement, you lose touch with the body's natural clock. Me, I love this time of morning. I've always done my best thinking between three and seven before anyone else is up."

Perhaps it was the time of day or the absence of ceremony that accompanied my less than vigorous state upon waking, but as I lay there inviting recovery, I asked, very quietly, if he would tell me how he had met Katherine Waddell, and what—if he did not find the question overly presumptuous—was the nature of his relationship to her. He asked me if I had some time to spare: it was a long and involved story. I had only to turn my head and look at him, gingerly lest I set into motion that which threatened to remain perpetually so, to let him know I was his willing audience. My only plea was that he speak softly.

Fessenden's mother's father, Edward Trenholme, lost his fortune many times to "the inventing game," as she called it with no small amount of derision, and so from the earliest hints that Reginald wanted to spend his life pulling machines apart and learning to make newer, better ones, Clementina Fessenden did everything she could to dissuade him, including locking him in his room at night to prevent him from sneaking into his father's study to read. He found a way to escape. He would have been four or five then.

His father was the Reverend Elisha Fessenden, an impecunious Anglican minister who found it difficult to see God's shining light through the clouds of his poverty and depression. The year Reginald was born, his father had a church near Sherbrooke, Quebec, where Reginald's mother had grown up, and within sight of the ruins of his grandfather's failed woollen mills on the St. Francis River. It was as if the seeds of his father's personal ruin were already there in the water and the air, his mother's dour, practical nature letting him know early: if you try to reap something out of nothing, you will reap less than nothing; you will lose that which you already possess. In Elisha's case it was his life, by his own hand. The inventor admitted that not until that very moment when he told his story to me had he thought to equate what his father did with what he had spent his life attempting to do, which was to harness the secrets of the natural world for the betterment of humankind. Yes, he said, his mother was right. They were both of them, he and his father, trying to create the illusion of making something where there had previously been nothing. I think that of the two of them Elisha had the harder task—to conjure the Holy Ghost and summon faith in the invisible.

Relocations every few years, as much as did the niggardly poverty, wore Elisha down. How was he supposed to build a congregation when he had to uproot his family every few years? How was he supposed to draw the timid and suspicious doubters out of their farmhouses without time to wait and be seen and let the word of his ministry bubble to the surface of the ploughed fields?

From his earliest memory Reginald had no patience for waiting. His father waited for God to speak to him, but the boy refused to wait. He vowed to go out and find God in the earliest places of His tenancy on Earth, to pull back the curtain to expose that which had once been real and which time had shrouded in myth. He believed that we have but a single myth and that is that there are phenomena that cannot be explained. Only someone as well schooled in scripture and ancient texts as he, taught by a strict, passionate, doomed, flawed man desperate for just one sign of the divine, could make such a sacrilegious claim.

Reginald was the eldest of four boys. By the time he was ten he had taken apart his father's clock in the minister's study and had built an insulated box so that he could throw snowballs at girls in June. He could not remember whether or not he had reassembled the clock so that it kept proper time. "I may well have," he said. "I hope I did!" He took his mechanical ability for granted, just as he never questioned his ever-present desire to know how things worked. How did birds fly and why could we not? Why did sound travel farther at night than during the day?

Elisha was given a new church near Niagara Falls, and after a brief stint at an American military school, Reginald became a boarder at Trinity. There he met Archibald Lampman, who was five years older than he was, as were most of the other boys. Archie, as he liked to be called, did not see their age difference to be an obstacle to their friendship, and he further endeared himself to the new arrival by not making fun of Fessenden's thick glasses. By Reginald's way of thinking, they could be of some use to each other. He could coach Lampman through mathematics, and his literate friend could reciprocate by helping him with English literature. They were equals in the classics. Lampman proved to be a good friend who did not judge, although they saw the world through wildly different eyes: Archie refused to isolate any one aspect of experience at the expense of the whole, and Reg was forever doing just that, bringing his magnifying eye close to the minutiae of a phenomenon, trying to see deep into the fabric of it. "Leave it be" was his motto; Reg's, "Make it better." How early set is the plastic mould of the mind.

At Trinity they became interested in the similarities between accounts found in different ancient traditions. Had he not been so hell-bent on inventing, Fessenden might have devoted his life to uncovering the answers to those nagging echoes in the various texts. Nevertheless, as he lay abed unravelling his story, he believed that he was close to an answer, and that what he sought lay in the shadow of those same mountains towering over us.

Archie liked it best when they left off debating the role of science in human progress and took up where they had left off in what they referred to as the Puzzle. "Casaubon in *Middlemarch* was working on the very thing as we are," he would say, "the key to all mythologies," and would tell Reg all about the various affairs and intrigues in the novel. Fessenden had no interest in reading a novel that size but did recall being told that Casaubon died a dried-up old prune of a man, mired in details, having lost sight of the larger structure of his work. "You're being a Casaubon," Lampman would scold, whenever he thought his friend was dwelling too long on a particular point.

"But I had to, you see, Henry. To my mind it all hinged on one thing—geographical amnesia."

I asked him to explain what he meant by the term.

"Well, the forgetting begins with language. Change the meaning of a single word, and a fact can become so obscured as to be almost irretrievable. This did not happen often, the Greeks taking every precaution to translate myths accurately, word for word. For heaven's sake, the Spartans handed Salamis to the Athenians on the evidence of a single line of myth! These were not people who made it up, as they say. Thus, when we see changes—I prefer to call them errors—in myths and omens, these happen invariably because the meaning or pronunciation of a word has changed. For example, we are told that the oracle at Dodona was founded by three pigeons."

The image made me laugh aloud, despite my feeling ill.

"I assure you, that is what the account, as translated today, says. Real pigeons, clay pigeons, stool pigeons, *pigeon bleu*?—I don't know. My best guess is that the oracle had been founded by three elders, *palaiai*, three syllables, but in time the word came to be pronounced *palaai*, with only two syllables. The person reciting the myth could not change the number of syllables in the line, the whole story being in verse and following the strictest rules of meter, and so he was understood as saying *peleiai* or pigeons, the closest word. When the myth was finally written down, the error became permanent, at least until someone understood what had happened."

"Very well, but how does such amnesia become geographical?"

"The Greeks, like you Brits, were great travellers and colonisers for the purpose of trade, but unlike the British they were in the habit of losing touch for long periods of time with their customers. Sometimes other sea powers blocked the route, or a commodity might be easier obtained from someplace else, or the customer nation or colony itself might have ceased to exist because of war, famine, earthquake, pestilence, or the like, and the only record that there was such a place and such a route to get to it would be the myth preserved in the home temples. Strabo tells us that when the Phoenicians lost touch with the Colchians, inhabitants of the eastern shore of the Black Sea, they looked in vain for the Pillars of Hercules, which marked the entrance to the Ocean of Atlantis. They had faithfully kept a record of the route but failed to find the Pillars.

"Archie thought that the stelae—massive columns, one of brick, the other of marble, one topped with a red, the other a yellow or green light, depending on who is writing—had crumbled to dust, but I didn't believe that was so. The ancients built their monuments to last. It was their best way to preserve knowledge, and only if the columns were exposed to water or the eroding effects of high desert winds might they deteriorate quickly. No, it was not the Pillars of Hercules—and this was not a reference to the mythical hero but to an earlier figure, a more ancient god—not they that disappeared, but the Sea of Atalontas, the original Atlantic Ocean. For this is what happened. It is so simple as to make one doubt himself, but here it is. Across this isthmus came a great inundation. Like a war machine it came, obliterating everything in its path. There was warning enough, however, that one man—call him Noah or Atra-Hasis—had time to build a great vessel. Perhaps he built a fleet of arks, who can say for certain? In any case, after the floodwaters subsided, there were survivors. Some stayed, settling high in the mountains to avoid a similar disaster, but most took what they could carry and began the exodus in every direction. They took with them names from the original land—Iberia, Crete, Libya, Eden, Acheron, the River Styx. Those who settled in what is now Spain, for example, called the great body of water to the west the Atlantic, and searched unsuccessfully around the Strait of Gibraltar for the Pillars. I believe that the entire block of land stretching between Greece and the Iberian Peninsula has been in a sense misplaced in our consciousness and has been given a designation belonging originally to this land, what we now call the Caucasus.

"Let me put this to you—why did Hercules, returning to Tiryns with the oxen of Geryon, setting off from Gades and the Pillars of Hercules, pass through the country to the north of the Black Sea? Why does Mount Atlas in Libya hardly resemble its description in the myths? How is it that the Argonauts, after entering the mouth of the Danube, passed through Egypt, of all places, on their way to the Adriatic?"

I was no help in answering his questions.

"Surely you find it as intriguing as I do—it must have been no end of disturbing to the Greeks—that in the older myths the routes supposed to have been taken on certain expeditions cannot be reconciled in any reasonable way with the known geography? The accounts of mythic expeditions in the first and last legs of the routes always make sense, and any inconsistencies with known geographical facts are always consistent with each other. If the travellers set out for a destination in the far west, Hyperborea, for example, or the red island Erythia, or the islands of the Hesperides in the so-called Atlantic Ocean beyond the Pillars of Hercules, they always first went east, into the Black Sea and along its shores to the Caucasus, and then, miraculously, popped up in the Atlantic Ocean after a fuzzy description of the route. The adventurers did whatever they had set out to do, retrieving the golden apples of the Hesperides or the oxen of Geryon, and then, after another vague itinerary, followed the shore of the Black Sea home to Greece. We have members of the same family living, some in the far east, others in the far west, but with no explanation for the separation. Prometheus was in the Caucasus, we are told, with Echidna and Typhon in the general vicinity, but Prometheus's brother, Atlas, and the Hesperides, his nieces, along with Geryon,

Echidna's brother, and Orthus, son of Echidna and Typhon, lived beyond the Pillars of Hercules, the exit to the Atlantic Ocean. Despite this separation, we are told that they were all in regular communication. I challenge you to explain, using a modern map, how that could have been so. Oh, but there is so much more, I hardly know where to go next.

"Atlas—Mount Atlas, sometimes placed here in the Caucasus, but usually on the shore of the Atlantic. The country of the Hyperboreans, sometimes in the far west, sometimes not far from the Black Sea. Many of the myths take place east of Sicily and west of the Caucasus, and many are set in the Atlantic Ocean, but none is set between Sicily and the present Atlantic Coast. Not one. I have checked it exhaustively.

"I believe that the early myth tellers such as Homer and Hesiod had no idea where Spain or the present Atlantic Ocean were. Knowledge of that part of the world did not reach the Greeks until several hundred years after Homer was dead. Their expeditions were invariably oriented eastward, toward the rising sun rather than following a dying one. When I examined the places in the Atlantic Ocean that supposedly correspond with those in the myths, I was inevitably disappointed. The island that is supposed to be Erythia isn't red. The supposed Gades has notoriously bad water, contrary to the tradition. Mount Atlas is relatively low and far from the shore."

I interrupted him. "But shorelines change, do they not? And freshwater sources dry up or become contaminated over time."

"You're right. Nevertheless, I am hardly the first to ask

these questions, sir. The later Greeks were similarly puzzled by these inconsistencies. The tradition says that the Atlantic was relatively shallow and shoal and unnavigable opposite the Pillars of Hercules, and was surrounded entirely by land. Does that sound like the Atlantic beyond Gibraltar to you?"

I admitted that it did not.

"We kept stumbling, Lampman and I, over curious one-to-one correspondences between points on the eastern shore of the Black Sea and on the western shore of the Mediterranean. In the east, in the Transcaucasus, Iberia stretches from the Black Sea to the Caspian. In the west, in Spain and Portugal, Iberia is similarly bounded by two bodies of water, the Atlantic and the Mediterranean. Both Iberias are bounded on the north by high mountains running from sea to sea, east and west, and in both ranges there is a Mount Atlas. In the east, Hypanis. In the west, Hispalis and Hispania. Aragon and Aragus. Such close pairings of names abound. The country about the mouth of the Danube and inland was called Libui. In the west we have Libya. It was as if someone had tried to duplicate, on the other side of the known world, every inch of an intimate landscape.

"Only one explanation made sense. There must have been on the eastern edge of the Caucasus a body of water large enough to be called an ocean but surrounded entirely by land. Such an ocean did exist. It is known to geologists as the Asiatic Mediterranean, the original Atlantis, and existed as late as the time told of by the myths. It spread some 1,850 miles from the

Caucasus to Mongolia, about the same distance as from, say, Liverpool to Come by Chance, Newfoundland, and its eastern portion was probably connected at one time with the Arctic Ocean. All that is left of it now are the Caspian, the Aral, and the Balkasch Seas, the last remaining parts that have not yet dried up. As late as 200 B.C., the Caspian and the Aral were still connected. We know that merchandise from India was being brought by boat from Faisabad to Sura in the Caucasus Valley around that time. Strabo tells us that the Caspian was connected to the Black by way of the Sea of Azov, at whose mouth I believe archaeologists will find one pair of the Pillars of Hercules. The connection was by way of the Manytsch Lakes. Geologists confirm it.

"Once we accepted that the Atlantic—Atalontas—was a huge inland sea, the mythic itineraries began to make sense. Hercules drove the oxen of Geryon back along the northern shore of the Black Sea because it was shorter than the southern route, had good pasturage and good water, and was relatively level. To have gone by the southern shore would have meant going through Erebus, this same pass where we are sheltered, and which at that time did not have the convenience of a modern military road. In short, it was virtually impassable for cattle, and even if Hercules had made it through, the southern shore of the Black Sea was and still is mountainous.

"Similarly our hero Hercules's expedition for the apples of the Hesperides presents no difficulty, for now we have Atlas—Mount Elbruz—in sight of Mount Kasbek, to which

Prometheus was chained, and at the foot of Kasbek was the Garden of the Hesperides.

"Suddenly it made perfect sense that the Argonauts sailed back by the north shore of the Black Sea to the mouth of the Danube, up the river, through the labyrinthine channels of the Balta system, which was Lake Tritonis of the myth, up the Save and Kulpa to above Karlstadt, and from there portaged a short distance through the country of the Libui or Illiberi, and finally out into the Adriatic. From there they sailed south along the eastern shore of the Adriatic to Greece. This was a well-used path of commerce between the Black Sea and northern Italy. It avoided the long journey through the Dardanelles, the way you sailed in coming to Novorossik, and around Greece with its heavy tolls and threats of pirates. Such a route would have been onerous for the Argonauts, who were on the run, as it were, having murdered the son and abducted the daughter of Aeetes, the king of Colchis. The Colchians, who were the original black Phoenicians, the Aethiopians of Ephorus, and who had colonised Egypt, had a large fleet of ships in the Black and Aegean Seas. The Argonauts would never have been able to escape their pursuers via the Dardanelles route, and so they followed the Iberian trade route, up the Danube."

"Remarkable!"

"Yes, so it is. It represents years of study and conjecture."

They did not get very far with it before Archie graduated and went off to Toronto to university. They corresponded for a few years. He taught school, moved to the civil-service job in Ottawa, was married to Maud Playter, a young woman who used to take singing lessons from his mother in the Lampman family parlour, published his poetry here and there, but became increasingly bitter at his lack of literary recognition. His letters to Fessenden became fewer and fewer until years passed without the inventor hearing from him. Then some months ago he heard from Maud that Archie had died. He wasn't yet forty years of age.

It was Archie who first suggested that the myths of the ancients had to come from some wellspring of the actual. You had only to look at his face and see truth shining there, said Fessenden. Lampman could neither lie nor knowingly hurt another living thing. He was in touch with something akin to the divine, a force the two men interpreted differently. Life to the poet was infinitely interconnected. The death of one being—and he lumped ant, elephant, man, paramecium all together—profoundly weighed upon the life, the balance as it were, of all others. He was the most naive man Fessenden had ever known, if in fact one can know another mainly through his writing. In this I include Lampman's poems along with his letters, because they are works of great craftsmanship that reveal his heart as truly as any confession of the soul. And by "naive" I think Fessenden meant someone who placed himself, as much as he could, outside of those worldly concerns that harden us to the sanctity of the natural world, to love, and to the conservation of all that is good. The professor believed that his friend stopped writing to him because he could not accept

Fessenden's belief in the renewing power of human ingenuity. We are limited, he said, only by our ability to think original thoughts and to use the resources of the world in new ways and to find new resources to exploit. Lampman refused to be open to this way of thinking. "You would dam all the rivers," he wrote. "You would clear Algonquin Park, if you had your way."

"No, you're wrong," Fessenden wrote back to him one of the last times they corresponded. "The forest in Algonquin is of little interest to me because the trees there take too long to grow back to maturity and there is no easy way to get them out. That I'll leave to the lumber kings. Now, as for the trees along the upper Ottawa River, there's another story altogether," and that sparked another exchange of volleys via the post.

It's funny, sad, actually, that Lampman should have mentioned Algonquin Park that time, because he loved it there and it was on a canoe trip deep into it that he contracted the pneumonia that finally led to his death. He wrote that when he was paddling through lakes so still you could hear the sound of the water striders skating along the surface, he saw creation's plan in its entirety, but that when he tried to capture it in verse it fled from his mind. That is how he knew it was divine: words could not be made to fit.

The professor admitted that he had talked at length but had said nothing in answer to my original question. How had he come to meet Miss Waddell?

"A simple answer really," he said. "It begins with a response to a man's final request. Lampman, an invalid dying of congestive heart failure complicated by pneumonia, said to her, 'Kate, my darling, when I am gone, take what is left of me to Eden. Reg will know how to get there. Find him and convince him to take you.' And so she did."

It was simple enough for her to track him down from Lampman's correspondence. Such an unusual request: take me with you to the seat of all mythologies. It never occurred to her that Fessenden had no such an expedition planned, that he was content to publish his obscure studies and leave it at that. You might say she ambushed him with her request. Previously content to point to places on a map and suggest to archaeologists that they dig there, he was now being asked to lead the way, and by a young woman he had never met and had barely heard of before the day she showed up at his office door. Their reasons for travelling to the Caucasus were as different as an Armenian is in temperament from a Georgian, and yet they converged. For were they not seeking what any traveller seeks in this life, the same rest, the same heaven-in-knowledge? She, to carry out the wishes of the man she loved and thereby, perhaps, to glimpse the portal through which his soul would pass on its way to the next life. He, to stand on the peak of Mount Tamischeira, imagining himself there with the women of the Chalybes—the Amazons, their queen among them—feeling the terror of the earthquakes, watching as the tidal wave like a monstrous engine of war swept past below them over the plain to drown every last one of their men. The thought of it, he admitted, was a manacle on his imagination ever since she came to him that day. That he might stand on the soil of the first great civilisation on Earth, that he might see the mythical places as they really were. The miracle for him was to embrace the reality of it; for her, the poor, distraught girl, it was to be reunited with her lover, wherever and in whatever form that may be.

"Truly, Mr. Norman, I despair for her safety and have kept an ever closer watch on her as we draw closer to Eden."

Fessenden continued to talk for an indeterminate length of time as I drifted in and out of sleep, his words in the conscious air between us, now blending with my dreams. My plan for that morning had been to rise early and before breakfast climb to a tiny and ancient chapel high above us, my intention being from there to enjoy an uninterrupted view of the spot on the mountain where Prometheus is believed to have been chained. Fessenden, ever straining for the scientific explanation, believed that Prometheus was punished for stealing not fire itself but naphtha, the fuel that lay so close to the surface there.

When I finally did pull myself off the lumpy cot, I was alone in the room. The world outside had been transformed into one of downy white. Even the imperious camel, who I learned had a counterpart at each station along the route of the pass, was blanketed in snow. He was there to make the horses familiar with his kind so that they might not be spooked should they encounter any of the caravans that make their way in both directions between Europe and Asia, but on this morning he looked like a ghost and would have frightened the most courageous lion.

The professor was standing in an agitated state outside and was trying to make himself understood in his broken Russian to the station master and his wife. Between us we learned that both Katherine and Sergei were gone, that they had ridden off on horseback before first light. The keeper's wife had woken in the night to relieve herself at her chamber pot—the man lingered unnecessarily over the details, much to the chagrin of the woman—and it had been then that she had noticed Miss Waddell's absence from the bed. Hearing sounds coming from the stable, she hurried outside, where she found her son, who groomed the horses and who slept in an annex attached to the barn. She saw two figures astride a single horse disappear around a bend in the road. The boy recounted what had happened.

A man—undoubtedly Sergei by the description—had been making a racket by stomping his feet and cursing at the top of his voice as he tried to pull a horse from its stall. The couple performed this scene in pantomime for us. The horse, played by the stolid wife, would have nothing of it. The man was in the midst of cutting at the animal with a whip when the boy, now awake to the commotion, intervened and spent the next few moments calming the horse and its mates in the stalls nearby. The man told him to saddle the horse and to get food and a rifle, threatening to do him great harm if he did not comply. The boy did what he was told without question, trained as he was to obey his superiors instantly. Throughout all this the young woman stood anxiously outside the stable door. I have no doubt the boy had noticed Katherine as she sat at supper and perhaps had become infatuated with her from a distance as he caught glimpses of her through windows and doorways. He was probably watching as she whirled ever faster during the frantic, intoxicated dance, her back and her face flashing alternately before him, while to me she was motionless, her radiant face a portrait hanging in the air. He saw her take a few steps backward in the fluffy snow while Sergei wrestled with the frightened mare he meant to ride. Katherine turned and looked toward the entrance to the dining hall, hesitating as if unsure of her next move. The man said something loudly and sharply in her language. It had the sound of an order, and when she heard it she came just inside the barn and watched while the boy readied the animal.

They mounted, the man in front, the woman behind, her skirts gathered to allow her to straddle the horse's back, her arms encircling his body, when the groom returned with bread, sausage, a skin of wine, and a rifle. The wind was picking up, whipping snow into their faces. The man was no better dressed for riding than was the woman, for neither had the proper boots or trousers. The woman pulled her shawl over her head against the snow, but the man went bareheaded, a point neither of the interpreters of the event could fathom, for this was the first of the winter's snow, arriving in September and not leaving before April. Sergei dug his heels ruthlessly into the horse's unprotected flanks, and they sped off at a gallop.

"Which direction?" we demanded.

Upward, they pointed, toward Mount Kasbek, in the same direction we had been heading.

We set out to follow their trail as best we could, but a single horse travels faster and farther through deep snow than does a heavy carriage, neither of us being experienced horsemen. Barely out of sight of the station house we became stalled, the vehicle sinking to the height of its axles, and we trudged back to see what alternative transportation might be afforded us. By the time a horse-drawn sled large enough to accommodate two additional passengers had arrived, the entire day had passed, and we had no choice but to wait until morning, the driver, travelling alone, unmoved by our explanation that a woman's honour if not her very life was at stake. Without Sergei to translate, we could not make him understand the urgency of our entreaty.

As the pass continued to fill with snow, we sat in the dingy eating hall before a greasy meal made doubly inedible by worry. That night we occupied the same beds in the same dormitory where the professor had told me of his intriguing theories concerning this land that now felt like a prison. In the morning the trail was cold. No one we asked and were able to communicate with remembered seeing a man and woman together on horseback. I suspect that such a sight elicits only the most romantic of feelings in those who witness it: a man and woman riding bravely through the night toward their life together. Undoubtedly they were lovers escaping families who opposed their union. Perhaps they flew toward some powerful, benevolent prince who would give them asylum. Perhaps, as I believed was the case, the bounder had kidnapped her and would force his will upon her in the most unspeakable way. Even that I felt, as I examined the faces of the mountain peasants we interrogated, was a union to cheer and to hide from foreign interlopers like us.

When the professor and I reached Tiflis, we alerted the authorities to the circumstances surrounding Miss Waddell's disappearance and gave a description of Borshelnikov. We renewed our pledge to do all we could to find her. After all, he reminded me, Katherine Waddell had been the one to rouse him from his comfortable berth in academe and convince him to make the voyage. Only he more than I could make the legitimate claim that he was responsible for Miss Waddell's safety, and I believed that if anyone could bring about her recovery he was the man to do it.

With the approach of winter it became too difficult to continue our search in the mountains, and we agreed to return in the spring. We had few leads. One, the account of a Persian merchant who had talked briefly with a couple whom he had encountered on the Caspian route into Daghestan, seemed to hold some hope. The description he gave of the man did not fit that of Sergei, but the woman was undoubtedly Katherine. The place to begin would be the capital, Makhach-Kala. In the interim Fessenden was invited by the Russian government to observe the oil-drilling operation in Baku and to advise representatives of the companies there about ways of increasing their efficiency.

I returned for the opening of the fall session of Parliament, and while I tried to lose myself in the work of various committees, many of which addressed bills meant to provide relief to the poor, my mind continually drifted back to the Caucasus. The unfinished business there seemed so much more urgent than anything I was doing at Westminster. How could I be so far away and so ineffective while Katherine Waddell remained unfound and in peril? I let myself think the unthinkable, which only steeled my resolve to return as soon as possible to resume the search.

When the House broke for the spring recess, I returned to Baku, where I found Fessenden helping inept oil men to extract the plentiful black gold from the ground without so many of the delays that traditionally hampered their progress. I arrived at night, a lurid glow from the petroleum furnaces illuminating a forest of wooden derricks, thousands upon thousands of them standing with only a yard or two separating them. The air reeked of burning oil, the roar of the furnaces and the pounding of the augers incessant and deafening. Surely this was as close to Hades as a soul could come on Earth. I covered my face with my handkerchief in order to breathe. Between the rickety wooden pyramids, many of which were shaking with the tremendous force exerted by the digging tools, was a network of black canals designed to contain the runoff, and pipes going every which way to transport the oil to storage reservoirs.

I found Fessenden inside one of the derricks. He looked dreadful, his face smeared with dirt and grease, his eyes betraying months of sleeplessness, and yet when he saw me he smiled broadly as if I were a long-lost brother.

His delight, I soon learned, stemmed not only from seeing his travelling companion again. During his tenure in the oil fields as a technological adviser, he had helped improve the extraction process to such an extent that he halved the time that normally passed between first strike of the auger to the pumping of clean oil. Many of the oilmen, working independently on their own little plots, were using a process that was thirty years old. In it a free-falling auger dug and a baler removed the earth, and then lengths of iron pipe were lowered into the resulting hole. The wider the shaft, the larger the baler, an elongated bucket that eventually brought the oil to the surface, and thus the greater the yield and associated profit each day. It made me think about the poor of my constituency again, disenfranchised by hunger, and I wished they all had a tiny oil derrick of their own pumping bread and happiness into their mouths.

The problem put to him was one he attacked with his characteristic vigour and imaginativeness. The digging tools, the spades and balers and their assorted attachments, along with the shaft tubes themselves, were forever breaking and getting stuck in the hole. Spades cracked in two, pipe shafts collapsed under the weight of tons of rock bearing down upon them, steel cables snapped, sending the whole beam apparatus crashing down, or the auger would get stuck deep in the shaft. Around these predictable difficulties an entire profession, that of oil borer, had grown. Usually the oil borer would be called upon, as one would summon a plumber, to remove some object that had fallen into the well; even something as small as a lug nut could bring the entire operation to a halt. Often the blockage was a mass of broken, twisted iron rendered immovable in the narrow space, with a long snarl of metal rope or chain heaped on top of it. With an assortment of instruments resembling the dental tools of an ogre, this petroleum surgeon set about to effect the necessary extraction. Each tool weighed hundreds of pounds, and it could sometimes take the oil borer months to clear a blockage, all the while working blind with only the feel of the instrument dangling at the end of a wire a quarter of a mile below to guide him.

Although he was unable to retire the position of oil borer, his contribution to the industry dramatically reduced the need for the expert extractor. His innovation was to replace the clumsy free-fall auger with a drill so hard and so persistent that it cut through the most obstinate rock and lifted it to the surface in cylindrical cores. He also introduced a continual flow of water to the shaft as the diamond-studded drill did its work, cooling the operation and reducing breakage. Instead of the beam engine driving the digging apparatus as one might drive a pile into the ground, the drill shaft rotated at high speeds, and because the drill had to be removed less often, the number of jams and blockages became fewer. In short, by the time I arrived to witness the testing of his new system, he was well on the way to making his commissioners rich men.

But that, as I have intimated, was not the only reason he was overjoyed. Aside from making the oil fields of Baku flow as they had never before, he had made a discovery in analysing some of the core samples his drill had brought to the surface.

"That, Henry, that line. Tell me what that is."

I shook my head.

"The Deluge, man, the Great Flood. It might as well be stamped with the words. It came with the violence of the gods, and it receded, leaving a fine thick silt over all."

Each year the administrative budget of Daghestan was sent under protective convoy from Russia to Makhach-Kala, the state capital, the spot where we agreed we should resume our search for Miss Waddell. That spring, when the heavily armed convoy reached the town of Kislar, the colonel in charge of guarding the money received an anonymous letter telling him that the convoy would be attacked. His response was to lock the money in a vault, post an around-the-clock guard, and wait a week before proceeding. During that time, he was visited by a dignified-looking man claiming to be a prince (in truth, it seemed as if every fourth person in the Caucasus was a prince), who reinforced the warning of the letter: the moment the convoy set out for Makhach-Kala word would spread, and when the colonel least expected it, armed *abreks* would sweep out of the hills to overwhelm his force. There was nothing the prince could do to prevent it. He advised, therefore, that the colonel send for reinforcements. The next day another unsigned letter addressed to the Russian officer repeated the dire warning, and in communicating with his counterpart in the capital he learned that similar rumours abounded there also.

The colonel waited until an additional troop of a hundred soldiers joined his brigade and then, in a show of force, began to move the gold toward its destination. A trip that should have taken a day took many as the convoy halted in every town and village along the way. Prospective bandits, the colonel reasoned, should get a good long look at what awaited them if they dared leave the relative safety of the mountains.

Of course, the robbers never materialised on the road to Makhach-Kala. Instead, they drove heavy wagons into Kislar at their leisure and stripped the town bare. Not a shot was fired. I must admit that when we heard this story, Fessenden and I exchanged grins at the audacity of the scheme and its execution. We also had a feeling, after months of futile searching following tentative leads, a sighting here, a thirdhand story there, crisscrossing the entire width of the region many times over, that we were close.

We heard news of an incident in a village not far from Botlikh, and having no other thread to follow but our intuition, we decided to travel there. When we found Miss Waddell, she was much altered in dress and demeanour. She was brandishing a shovel with the other women of the village. Many were wailing as they broke ground. So familiar a sound; I had heard it in India, in Mexico, in the Basque region of Spain, and it haunts me still. We watched them fill the holes with the dreadful, shrouded packages, and cover them with lime and the accepting earth.

Part II

The north side of the Caucasus mountain range is relatively barren and deserted, the only signs of habitation the station posts along the route. But the south slopes are green. Quaint villages nestle protected from the north wind in fertile pockets. Into this verdant valley we rode, at times a wild rush at full gallop, the horse's hooves slipping on stones, skittering to catch up with its head as Sergei punished it on tight switchback curves.

The vegetation changed as we descended, stunted firs giving way to pines and scrub oak. Soon the vista opened into hay fields dotted with golden stacks drying in the open air. Here was no evidence of the snow that had made our passage so treacherous north of the summit of the Dariel Pass. On this slope we rode through tiny villages of dwellings built half underground, with square, open fronts that made me think of cave dwellings. The roofs were flat, and stacks of straw and mounds of winter fodder were heaped around them.

During a rest stop, I recalled one of Archie's letters from the woods. He and his companions had spent the day searching in vain for the elusive grey trout. One trapper, a wrinkled old leathery type with no teeth, told them that the grey had disappeared from his lake, and they were best to try the next one on. It was as if the old man had signalled ahead, because when they paddled and portaged to the lake indicated, another old trapper was there with thin lips and sunken eyes, and he said that the fish had gone to deeper waters to escape the heat. They should try the next lake in the chain, he advised, warning that they had no easy task ahead of them. The grey trout was a wise and tricky fish, one of the most difficult to snag. On and on the canoeists went, from one lake to the next, deeper into the bush until they thought they would never find their way back, yet still the fish eluded them.

Despite that failure, Archie wrote, there was beauty enough in the surroundings to console the most disappointed fisherman. "You must come here with me someday, Kate. I envision the two of us together, you in the bow and I in the stern steering our birchbark canoe. The lakes are pure, deep and dark. In the shallows at midday the brown water glows like burnished gold. The forest air tingles and the sun turns the morning mist into spirals of colour. At night the stars seem near enough to touch. I would teach you to answer the weird, disconsolate voice of the loon."

He was at peace there as he was nowhere else. The solitude rendered the men quiet and thoughtful, and each was loath to disturb the communion of another in that place of luxurious joy, that garden.

Sergei said that he knew where the souls of the dead must pause on their way through the underworld, and that he was taking me there. He told me that if we could catch the dead at just the right instant, we might pull the shade back into the land of the living. But for a night only, and he would be in spirit form, not flesh. I told him it would be enough for me. One last night.

He drove the horse at what felt to be an uncontrollable speed along the snowy road. I held on to him with all the strength in my arms and pressed my face against his back. The stable boy had found a thick woollen overcoat for Sergei, and for me a simple cape of the same material, which I tried to clasp around me. But I could not hold on to him and the garment at the same time, and so finally let it flap like an unfastened sail behind me.

We slowed and were at once surrounded by a troop of Cossack soldiers riding in the opposite direction. He told me to keep my face hidden. The heavily armed soldiers, probably returning from a campaign in Armenia, paid us little notice after Sergei spoke to them. I asked him what he had said to make them so uninterested in a man and woman on horseback at night in the first snowstorm of the season.

"I told them we were just married and are going to Tiflis for our honeymoon."

"I don't believe you."

"It's true! Very well, I told them that you were deathly ill and that I was taking you to a doctor and that they should avoid coming too close to you for fear of contagion."

I did not feel much like a bride but, cold and weary as I was, felt entirely, surprisingly well.

As we continued, the snow subsided and a half-moon appeared, making me feel feather-light and giddy. Mount Kasbek stood out now, cold and glittering against the bejewelled heavens. The road zigzagged upward, and at times the poor horse had to wade through drifts that reached to the top of its back. It was a docile, good-natured beast that wanted to please; had it not been so, it might have thrown us off its back and headed for safer parts, so jerky and rough was Sergei's handling of the reins and so deep the snow.

We rode through the night, and as the light of dawn began to reanimate the world beyond the path, we encountered an ox yoked to a snow plough clearing the way ahead. At certain points the road ran under sturdy overhangs made of timber already heaped with snow, and built to withstand the impact and weight of avalanches.

We climbed into morning. At the top of the pass a small cross stood out on the hillside to mark the summit, some eight thousand feet above sea level. It makes me short of breath and lightheaded even now to think about. The dizzying altitude, the thin air, the impetuousness of riding away from a warm bed into the night with a man about whose character I knew almost nothing. He was a lout but a lovable one, the way he pretended not to understand poor Henry, or bait him with his insubordination.

He had come in the night, whispering so not to wake the innkeeper's wife, ordering me to dress and to follow him, addressing me in a manner so common and familiar as to suggest that he knew my unspoken desires.

From my rooming house on Elgin Street I used to take the streetcar north to Sparks Street, where I would get off and enter what looked like a wooden shed. At the bottom of a long, boxed-in, unlit, creosote-smelling stairway one emerged on Besserer Street, and it was then that I would finally let out my breath. Here was Central Station, its ticket office, baggage rooms, unpainted plank platform with nail heads raised to snag our long skirts, and the tracks themselves. Some called it the Old Grand Trunk Station, although nothing about the terminus could be said to be grand.

The Rideau Canal spilled into the Ottawa River not far from there. Both Sparks and Wellington Streets spanned the canal, their bridges suggesting the rough apex of a V-shape. The dull yellow facade of the Russell Hotel caught the late-afternoon sun. I remember feeling longing and anger and hopelessness constricting my lungs, at that moment as likely to throw myself onto the tracks or into the oily murk of the artificial waterway as I was to throw my arms around Archibald's neck in greeting. The charming people in evening clothes were emerging from the Russell and the Alexandra Hotel—white kid gloves, top hats, fur stoles, cravats, overcoats, canes—on their way to dinner. Where? Government House perhaps, for an evening of music and cards. The governor general—would he even be there or would he be off chasing after the pretty little mink who had lately captured his heart? Ottawa was so uncomplicated, so varied in its modes of peacefulness, that even the adultery of the vice regent became part of the deeper fabric of the city's thrilling monotony.

I looked up and down the platform, relieved not to see Maud. Come, I conjured the iron horse, fire-breathing, smoke-belching dragon. Come, puncture this dank, hot, unmoving boredom. Like an arrow, arrive, hit, pierce to the quick. Make me forget, make me remember.

He was the first one off, jumping down while the train was still moving, spotting me, reaching me at a run. He was still wearing his voyageur clothes: heavy corduroy trousers, long-legged boots of oiled calfskin, red collarless flannel shirt open to the heat, and a scrap of rolled white cloth tied loosely around his neck.

He smelled feral from the bear grease he put in his hair and on his skin to ward off the biting flies. "Don't you want to go home to wash?" I asked him. No, he said. He was ravenous for the tavern food he had been thinking about all the way home: veal and ham pie, cold roast beef, pickles and seed cake and potted head and sausages rolled in paste, and pint after pint of Bass ale.

"What about me? Are you not ravenous for me?" I said with a put-on pout, and he engulfed me, bringing his mouth down hungrily to the bared skin of my neck.

As a cab took us east on Wellington over the canal, he told me about a conversation he had overheard on the train. An older couple, thirty years married.

He said, "When I heard, 'thirty years,' I wanted to scream out, 'No! Not so long a slow unwinding toward death as that! You and you, mister and missus, should long before this have exhausted your passion and parted, burned-out shells, wraiths, mere echoes of love.' But I sat and listened."

The man asked his wife if she remembered the night he proposed marriage to her and she said, "What do you think, that I would so carelessly forget such a night as that? You and your cronies had hired that hall for the dance, but you all drank too much whiskey, and when a rival bunch of river rats wandered in you couldn't help but brawl. I brought you home to my sister's and bandaged your head and you showed me the first dollar you ever made in timber. You said you'd never spend it."

"And where is it now?" he asked.

"You know as well as I. You spent it."

"I spent it on an orange to give to you."

"A whole crate of oranges," she said. "I never tasted anything so good."

"No," he said, "Just one. That's how rare they were. It only tasted like more."

And she said, "I still remember what you wore when we stood up together. It was that black suit with the Prince Albert coat that was my father's. The black had ever so slight a shade of green in it and you wore a boiled white shirt and a thin red tie made into a bow. I helped you tie it."

"You tied it for me," he said. "I was hopeless. Afterward we went for a walk along the river in the moonlight and you said, "You don't have that dollar anymore, but now you have me."

I kissed him then. I didn't care what he smelled like or whether or not he had finished telling the story.

The Saints' Rest was set in behind a high wooden fence so that you couldn't see it from the road. The cab entered through a narrow gate and dropped us at the door. It sounded as if four different songs were being sung inside the tavern, none of them in key. Light spilled out the open door. Why here? I wondered. Why not the Russell or the Alexandra? He's ashamed of me. He can be anonymous here. But as soon as the petty thought was out I dismissed it. We were anonymous here and we weren't; it was a matter of degree. All I cared about was that we were together. The cabby and the innkeeper and the barmaids and the soused patrons could wink all they liked. Here we had no need for the despised calling card, the pretence of society, the "climbers." I vowed I would take the Saints' Rest over Rideau Hall every time, eschewing skating parties, musicales, tired gossip, and sterile chat about Who Saw Whom

Going Where Dressed in What.

What I wanted, desperately at that moment, was touch, breath, the feel of his tongue alive against my own, his heat and scent, the taut, elastic give of his muscles. After weeks of canoeing, his shoulders were like polished wood, his forearms grooved, rope-like, the skin burnt by the sun and redolent of wood smoke.

We were brought to an upstairs room taken up by a bed and a bathtub. Two men came and filled the tub with hot water from buckets. We locked the door. How had I contrived to continue living while he was away? I wanted time to stop while we were there in that ugly little room, that paradise. We fashioned a slick upon the water made of our urgency, a froth of soap, the bear grease, his spunk the instant I touched the trembling tip of him with my lips, and the thick river flowing from between my legs. The vapour off the surface of the water shrouded us, languorous, indolent. My heels resting upon his shoulders, my toes twiddling with his ears, his moustache. Then sudden insistence in his eyes as he pushed himself up, Poseidon rising from the deep upon a submarine volcano being born. He covered me, pressing against me. There was nothing to hold on to, everything was so slick. He turned me over onto my knees. Giddy, afraid, ambushed, half in the water, half out, draped over the end and—Zeus! Every inch of my skin gilded, tingling, the top of my head torn off. And again with no warning. Sweet death. Arms dangling, blood filling my head, magma flowing into my belly. Then collapse, stillness.

My heart or his? Spent carcasses in a carnal soup. Cooling potion, draining, all my bodily fluids, my tight plug popped and with it my red bloom, and he clasping me. "Hold on to nothing but me," he said, and I did. He smiled, stilled me as I shook, releasing: happy, inconsolable, embarrassed, ecstatic, frightened by the depth to which we dived, breathing for each other, the outer world hidden away behind walls of smoke-stained paper over plaster over latting over dumb stones of antiquity. We climbed out, dried ourselves. He called for more water, and they came, rolled the tub away, drained it into a hole in my memory, brought it back clean, and we rinsed off. O pungent scent, never again to be reproduced. I would have only to smell it once to die in ecstatic shudders, weeping, uncontrollably fitful, wracked by the remembrance of what we birthed, the sloshing overflow, the primordial mix. To drop the tip of my tongue to the surface again, to lap it as a cat laps her milk—please, gods, medicine men, charlatans, my life for that taste again, however brief. Give it. Give it up to me that I may take my leave of this life at last.

Archie's canoe trips and our secret meetings were only temporary escapes from the tedium of his life in Ottawa, and he clung to the hope of being offered a position, teaching at a university or editing a prestigious publication, commensurate with his literary abilities. Reginald Fessenden tried to arrange a year's exchange between a professor, who was going to be on sabbatical and who had expressed an interest in living in Canada, and Archie.

Crestfallen, Archie wrote to his friend: "Having heard nothing whatsoever from your Professor Broadhead, I can only conclude that the proposal has fallen through. Maud had herself quite worked up over the prospect, especially of living in the Broadhead mansion for a year. With domestic zeal the poor child had mapped out in her head virtually every detail of the transfer to Pittsburgh. I admit I am as disappointed as she.

"My fellow civil servants, having got wind of my intentions to 'desert my native country,' think me disloyal. They wax eloquent about 'Canada for Canadians,' but fail to see how much harder it is to get on in Canada than it is anywhere else, especially in the realms of the arts and academe. Oh, give me a British accent and all the tea and superior attitude that attends it, and I could take any position I wanted at McGill or Toronto. We remain profoundly suspicious of our own, and unless a man has gained recognition for his talent elsewhere, as you have, he must content himself with playing the second fiddle.

"Reg, You mustn't tease concerning a possible trip north. Should you arrange to take us in for a day or two, Maud and I would bask in the delight of being your hosts. Although luxury is not ours to offer you, I can give you spirited conversation and the company of one or two stalwarts able to keep the talk alive."

As we rode, Sergei told me that Pushkin—did he read no one else?—looked down into this same valley from the height of Mount Gut and named the different orchards as if he were naming his brothers and sisters. Beside us now ran the bright Aragva River, winding exactly as the Russian poet had said, "like a silver ribbon." Unlike Sergei and I, Pushkin had descended into the valley in the evening, noting a new moon punctuating the clear sky. The air was quiet and warm, as it was when first I breathed it.

We rode into Ananur in the early morning as the sun was rising. It became clear to me that Sergei knew nothing of the ancient spiritual lore attached to heavenly Georgia, for if indeed he was searching for a spot where the soul might logically rest on its passage through the underworld, then we had most likely passed it in the night. Instead we had arrived *there*, the desired Destination, what Reginald believed to be Eden. The valley was protected from the north wind by the great wall of the Caucasus and cupped on the remaining three sides by smaller ranges. Here, supposedly—and I wanted so to believe it—was the Garden of the Hesperides, whose location the ancients lost when, after the Deluge, survivors equated the east with terrible death and cast their gaze westward instead.

It frightened me less than I had expected it might to know I had willingly ridden into the black night with only starlight to illuminate our way, on the back of a horse commandeered by a man I knew to be a rogue. I had an idea what it was he really wanted with me. From the way he had crept into the bedroom I had been sharing with the station master's wife, waking me while at the same time placing his hand over my mouth, stifling my gasp of surprise and warning me of unspoken danger by putting a finger to his lips, he proved to be stealthy, calculating, commanding, and—I can say it now—exciting.

I went with him as much to escape the interminable boredom of the carriage as to experience some ghostly reunion with my departed love. I had found particularly vexing Reg's maddening silences while the incessant cogs of his brain turned, and Henry's priggish, self-important droning on about the exotic locales of his many travels. I took devilish delight in teasing Mr. Norman, discovering his Achilles' heel, tickling those points of ego that were sure to make him blush.

This, I believe, was the reason I had come to the Caucasus: to embrace danger and the promise of death, to be jolted out of lethargy and self-pity. For who was I? A former schoolmarm, a government clerk who most likely had no position to go home to, since I had left on my impetuous journey without securing the requisite permission. I was a widow who was not allowed publicly to mourn.

"Dear Reg, I must extricate myself from the quagmire of this job before much longer or I will surely turn into a desiccated corpse. The Canadian legislators, in their idiotic zeal to reform, have proposed to lengthen the civil-service workday, shorten the time allowed for lunch, and place veritable land mines in the way of anyone seeking to be granted a leave of absence. After changes such as these, what could possibly attract a man like me to the service of the country in this capacity? It is absurd. All this to convince the electorate that abuses of privilege and corrupt practices are being eliminated. I would love to burrow under the House of Commons when it reconvenes and plant a keg of dynamite. Band of rascals and cutpurses! Guy Fawkes had the glorious right idea. If I had my way, I would canonise him St. Guido, patron saint of poets condemned to drudgery. You are hereby warned: if any bits of Cabinet ministers came falling from the sky down there in Steel Town, you will know what has transpired.

"My man Tyler in Cambridge, Massachusetts, writes in a letter received some days ago that my interests there are being kept in mind and that he feels confident something will turn up for me before long. Certainly the critical reception that has attended *Among the Millet* will help in that regard. Something in his choice of words, however, keeps me from being entirely optimistic. There have been so many close calls. Yours, Arch."

When we began our love affair, we did our utmost to keep it secret. Usually one of us would leave the office first and begin walking east along Wellington Street and over the bridge slowly until overtaken by the other. If ever I was first, I would be all a-tingle with anticipation. I would try to muffle my steps the better to listen for his footfalls, which were light and quick, developed from many hours of treading silently along woodland trails, but many times his sudden touch at my elbow or his appearance ahead of me, hat tipped in greeting, smile escaping like a caged bird suddenly set free, would make me start. He took the greatest boy-like enjoyment from it.

"You almost made me scream!"

"I'll have to try harder tomorrow."

He walked backward a few steps, bouncing lightly on his toes, grinning. I let the look he loved, the one that said "What am I to do with you?" capture my face for a moment. Then he fell in beside me. At a bakery we bought a bag of sweet cinnamon rolls. We detoured through the market, where we purchased fruit and the afternoon edition of the Montreal *Gazette*. When we felt we were far enough away from the Hill, he gave me his arm, which I took, squeezing it with my gloved hand, and we walked thus joined, the single point of contact pulsing with communication.

"Why didn't you come to see me this morning?" he asked.

"Higgins has buried me with receipts to be recorded and filed. I think he knows."

"Who cares if he does. I'm sorry. I could just as easily have come to see you on some pretence or other. "Excuse me, Higgins, old bottom, but I need to borrow Miss Waddell for a bit. Seems there's an underground tunnel leading toward Parliament from the basement and I need her to carry the torch for me while I follow it."

"I'll carry your torch for you. Oh, yes, wouldn't that be appropriate—'Modern Day Guy Fawkes and Accomplice Found Blown Up by Own Bomb. Hansard Mistakenly Records Noise of Explosion as Rude Interruption of Government Speaker by Opposition Backbenchers!'"

We strolled south along the river. The air was cool, the leaves beginning to turn. We came to a white chapel and stepped inside. "Our church," we had come to regard it. We sat in a back pew, and I tore off pieces of sticky bun, feeding him, me, him again, a quiet, reverent ritual. When we finished eating, we sat in the cool cave of the sanctuary, aware of our time together as being a dying, guttering candle.

"Have you spoken to her yet?"

"I will. The moment...it hasn't been the right moment."

"You never will tell her. Husbands never leave their wives."

"I told you that I would. The baby has been ill the past few days. It wouldn't be fair to Maud. She's in a delicate state of health herself."

"They're going to cut our lunch hour in half. We'll barely have time to walk here in so short a time. Higgins is behind it, I know it."

"You know I can't support my family on my salary alone. Without Maud's inheritance..."

"She couldn't care if you wrote another line. You won't leave her because you're afraid of having to work hard enough at your writing to become successful at it."

He stood, indicating by taking his watch out of his waistcoat pocket that it was time to head back. The routine was that I would leave first, and five minutes later he would follow, keeping me in sight as best he could, a throwback, chivalrous gesture, the thought of which that day only made me angry.

"I think we should walk back together. There's so much more to say."

"You know we can't do that."

"You've been wanting to quit for months. I have some money put away. We could travel, finally see the Continent, as you've always wanted. Darling, think of it. We could see galleries and museums, attend readings and lectures. You could join a community of artists. We could teach English in Paris or Vienna or Florence. What holds you here? It's maddening to think of you stagnating in this provincial town that thinks it's bigger and better than it is. If you didn't want to stay in Europe to live, we could settle in Montreal. At least there you'd feel closer to your friends."

He began to fill his pipe as we lingered outside the church. With slow, deliberate movements he tamped me down, stopping my words with tobacco leaves fragrant of citrus peel and aromatic gum. He shouldn't have been smoking. He knew that; his lungs weren't up to it. I had urged him to stop countless times, but I wasn't thinking of his health now. He was shutting me out. For all his dreamy idealism he was a pragmatist, and for all his passion in word and touch he was still a son of the Protestant way, which had swung so far from rebellion as to be moribund.

And yet I could not part from this sickly, sad, stubborn, sweet man who would make of the world a garden and sit in it to the end of his days. Dreamer though he may have been, he was aware enough of the hard way of the world to see that he would never abandon his obligation to Maud, that social appearance meant much to him despite his derision, in essay and verse, of falsehood and mere show.

"You care too much what others think of you, when what you should care about most is whether or not you are doing justice to your art. Why are you so afraid? What is it you fear?"

Once the pipe was lit he was impenetrable. Instead of walking ahead of him, I took his arm. He removed my hand, had to pry it off. I raised my hand to strike him in frustration, leaving it there a second in the air, letting a ragged sound escape from my throat. I turned and went back into the church.

I did not return to work that afternoon or all the next day, a Friday, or the morning after that, sending word to Mr. Higgins each day in writing that I was too ill to come in. I suspect Archie feared I would lose my position. I was back Monday morning.

He gave me a book of handwritten poems that he said were about me. I told him I thought he had too fancy a vision of me. It was a beautiful book all bound in green. Perhaps he wrote them never intending for me to read them, for they were addressed not to the subject but to an unknown audience in a kind of confession. I believe they were his cry to be heard, to tell the world of his love for me.

The poems were what he saw in me, and I suppose they were no less real than the image I saw in my looking glass first thing each morning. I asked him to honour his vision, to uphold the validity of those words by acting upon them. Let them be not the anonymous confession of a man hiding from his fears, I urged, but the spur to a more public declaration. "Let me for once be the idealist, the impetuous voice of passion, dear man. Lean upon my strong limbs, for I would devote my life to you and your work if only you would let me."

He had said himself that art was a continual process of choosing, this hue over that, this angle of perception over another, this image over all others like it. Now I came to him with the audacious request that he make one more choice, not in his notebook but in the conduct of his life. He had said time and again that he loved me, that he no longer held feelings of ardour for his wife, and that Maud no longer believed, if she ever had, that making poetry was a worthwhile application of his time and talent. Whereas I did. I had never felt so strongly that a thing should happen, that he should be given the recognition, finally, that he deserved. From the moment I first heard him speak—did he remember reading from *Among the Millet* at the public library?—I knew I could help him.

"Allow me to be the helpmeet I was meant to be. Let us each not lose his life in regret."

In the last year of Archie's life, much sickness burdened the Lampman home. Their baby was ill with the croup again, and Maud, although not so stricken as the child, did not make as steady an improvement as she should have after her bout with the grippe. They arranged for Archie to board elsewhere for a few weeks and for a nurse to live in, to give some ease to Maud and, he hoped, accelerate her recovery.

He wrote to Reginald, again mentioning me, his "friend," who worked in the office with him. I shared with him the distinction of being a failed schoolteacher and a lover of poetry and art. "She is a kindred soul, and my regard for her grows daily. I trust you will use your utmost discretion and keep this revelation to yourself. Destroy this letter if you will; its existence after my death does not trouble me, however, and in time I believe my family will come to understand my love for this remarkable woman. To deny that love would be a sin, if indeed such a state exists. You continue to be one of my dearest friends, though distance and circumstance keep us physically apart, and I think of you as the receptacle of my every confidence."

Part of the letter has been destroyed, but it ends with a request of sorts, although I will never know for certain the details of that request. It is from a man undone by love who knew perfectly well that I was more than capable of taking care of myself, and yet he would not for all the world have me struggle after he was gone. "If this is not within your capacity to do, morally or otherwise, I understand and accept. There is no one else I can turn to, you see. This insidious flaw of mine, this damaged pump—how close I have come to stopping its erratic beat once and for all. Whatever your decision, tell me not. I'll ask only this once."

Sergei began pestering incessantly with demands that I marry him. I made it repeatedly clear: no, I was sorry, I could not, I did not love him. He grew dark, incommunicative. What might he do in his frustration? Had I been a fool to go with him?

In a little settlement, about midday, he procured some food and drink and said that we would be parting company, that he was sorry he could no longer be my guide and that he wished me well in my search for whatever it was I sought. I reminded him that I didn't know what it was I sought, exactly, and that I had been depending upon his knowledge in that mystical regard. He answered that, from this point onward, I would be in the hands of a new guide, a man named Assad, who knew the region and its mysteries far better than did he.

To say that I was gradually awakened from a stupor of ignorance in the next few hours is to suggest in the mildest of terms the extent to which I had been removed from all semblance of security. Believing Sergei's assertion that he was profoundly homesick and that he would be returning home, I gladly shifted my allegiance to Assad, a darkly complexioned, rudely handsome man with eyes that glinted like mica in the welcome bright light of Georgia. Just how unassuming I was in this transfer is evidenced by the fact that I did not question until much later Sergei's ability to pay Assad for his services as a travel guide.

I knew that he couldn't pay, but I suppose he didn't know that neither could I. My finances were scant. I had been depending upon Reginald and his funding from various scientific, historical, and geographical societies to cover all the expenses of the trip. I had my return ticket from England to Canada, my cigar box and its precious contents, my clothes, and a few British pounds sterling. How I would find my way to England or, once across the Atlantic, from Halifax, Nova Scotia, to Ottawa, I had not the vaguest notion. Strangely the absence of an itinerary had a liberating effect: I no longer cared where I went next, where I might be in an hour, a day, a year. For the first time since Archie's death, whenever I thought about him and the bounty of our short-lived love, it did not sadden me to contemplate my loss. I felt gradually relieved of grief, as if a tropical rain were pouring down, soaking, cleansing, purging.

I took the box out of my bag, which Sergei had snatched from behind the saddle and tossed at me angrily before riding away. I opened it. Inside were the mingled ashes of Archibald's letters to me and mine to him, with a lock of his hair he had let me cut the last time I saw him, bedridden at home, ashen, consumed by his disease.

"That's all you're going to get from me, my darling. No corporeal ashes to scatter in the Garden. Maud has made arrangements for a double plot in the Beechwood. I will spend all eternity with her lying beside me. She'll be so happy because I won't be able to write. God help me. You must try to find a way—" he wheezed, no strength to cough "—to get them to slip you in there between us when your time comes." I didn't want to hear him say such things and told him so. "Take those," he said, indicating a tied bundle of letters. "I've kept them safe. No one else has laid eyes upon them and no one will. If you still have mine to you—" I scolded him for suggesting I would have destroyed them "—then together these words are all the best of me. With them go my spirit, for it can't stay to haunt you, my precious Kate. You are too new and good and lovely to be someone who harbours ghosts. You will have many loves after me. It gladdens me to think of it."

I closed the box; this was not the right spot to release its contents. Sergei rode off on the horse, not in the direction we had come, for Henry and Reg would surely have caught him in the pass, but toward Tiflis. From there I imagine he went east in the direction of the Caspian, where he probably wheedled passage aboard a steamship heading north. He could travel in style now, given the price he got for me from Assad. It is a testament to my complete lack of awareness of my new "guide's" intent that I travelled with him until the end of the day before realising what had transpired between him and Sergei.

Assad spoke better English than Sergei, but far less often. I rode on the back of a donkey tethered behind his horse, and learned early that few of my questions—where we were, where we were going, what he knew about the history of the area—were going to be answered while we rode. I was wholly dependent upon his whim and had not the slightest idea what that whim might be.

We passed through Dushet, where the gleaming castle of Prince Tschliaief sat high on a hill overlooking a recently built Russian barracks. We had to cross the Kura River over an ancient stone bridge that was Roman in origin and which reminded me of Reginald saying, "Thus far and no farther." Those who had built the bridge, which stood in good repair two thousand years later, had yet been stopped in their advance at the foot of Caucasia.

As the day opened and we progressed, at a more leisurely pace than the one Sergei and I had beaten the night before, I drifted in and out of sleep, and once caught myself just before toppling off the donkey into the road. What men we saw were tall, brown-skinned from the sun, and heavily armed, with full bandoliers of ammunition slung over their shoulders. The women were slender and arrayed in bright colours, with blues and reds predominant, and their babies' hair was uniformly red, probably dyed with henna. Animals of all kinds clustered in the shelter of the house fronts: chickens, dogs, cats, the young of their domesticated buffalo. Corn dried on the rooftops in baskets the size of large shields, and often the head of the household would be sitting up there also, smoking a pipe and surveying his kingdom after harvest.

The last town on the Georgian Road before Tiflis was Mtskhet, the ancient capital of Georgia. We stopped there to rest and to water the animals, and it was there that Assad chose to inform me that I was to be his wife.

Perhaps my fatigue had got the better of me, but when he said this I began to laugh uncontrollably. I would have laughed at a funeral, I was so giddy from lack of sleep. I howled with it, clutched my sides for fear I would split open, gasped for air, and finally cried, a surprising, purgative release that went on and on.

He sat patiently on the grass where he had spread a blanket and upon it a simple meal of cheese, a round loaf of black bread, and a skin of Circassian wine. Finally he said loudly and sharply, "Enough!" and the shock of his voice silenced me.

I thought about where I was, how far from home I had been taken after Archie's death, what awaited me back in Ottawa. I was confident enough of my physical strength, once I had slept, and my persuasive powers, and my status as a citizen of the Empire, to believe that I could resist him in his insistence that I marry him and live the rest of my life—where? I did not know where we were going, where his home lay.

I reasoned that I could, if I had to, escape and take refuge in Mtskhet, the supposed oldest town in the world, founded by a great-great-great-grandson of Noah, and where all the tsars of Georgia had lived and reigned. Assad, when he did speak, was a font of knowledge. I never lost hope that Reginald and Henry would find me and take me under their protection home. I would resume my life, return to teaching perhaps, or see if I still had my old job. Could I pick up again at the point where I had dropped my life? Could I exist in

Ottawa without Archibald Lampman?

By way of answer I stood and emptied the contents of the box, and they settled by a light breeze a short distance away. I looked down into Assad's eyes. "Are you a good man? Will you treat me well?"

"I will honour you," he replied. "I can honour only Allah and my ancestors more."

"Will I be your only wife?"

He laughed and slapped his thigh. Standing, he faced me and took hold of me by the shoulders. "In Daghestan we are not like the Persians. We take only one spouse—for life."

"And will you allow me to go if I find I cannot live with you?"

"Yes, you will be free to go at any time. My family does not believe that a wife should be held against her will."

"The money you paid Sergei for me—I want you to pay me the same amount."

"I do not understand. You will want for nothing with me."

"You paid the wrong person. If you want me to follow you, then you must complete the transaction with the one who has the authority to act and speak on my behalf—me."

He looked as if he had taken on much more than he had been prepared to deal with. He may have been thinking that if he did pay me, then I was no better than a whore and that he would be unable to face me or keep me after that. Whatever he was thinking, he did not deign to let me know it.

On arriving in Tiflis, we went straight away to a bathhouse

owned by a man Assad knew, a Persian friend of his. The buildings of the city looked haphazard, all crowded together, flat-roofed and shuttered in the Asian style. Everywhere were donkeys burdened by pairs of deep panniers balanced one on each side and filled to the brim with trade goods, and ponderous oxen pulling heavy, creaking carts through the steeply inclined, narrow streets.

At the bathhouse we were shown to a large, open room where women of all ages were standing, undressing, or getting dressed in a sonorous choir of lively yammer and chat. At first I thought that Assad had inadvertently been led to the women's changing room, but he was not in the least embarrassed to be in the midst of so much unclad female flesh, and I saw that the room was meant to be a communal facility. It was Tuesday, the owner explained, Ladies' Day, and neither were any of the fifty or so women fazed by the presence of a naked man in their midst.

I took my cue from him, casting not a few surreptitious glances at his lean, well-muscled limbs, and feeling a powerful stirring of desire and strange unease as I disrobed. We sat as a continually evolving congregation in a steam room where, at first, I could hardly draw a breath, the air was so superheated with moisture, and I stood to leave. A woman gently took my arm and bade me sit again, this time on a bench closer to the floor until I became used to the temperature, and she began, unbidden but also unbarred by me, to rub an aromatic oil into my skin. I closed my eyes and tried to place the aroma.

Sandalwood? Jasmine? Rose water? What was it? Perhaps all three mingled in a rapturous scent. She directed me to lie down on my front on the wooden tier and receive her expert hands, which worked with strength and gentleness into the deep, locked places of my body.

The chatter of the women receded, though nothing in the room, no signal generally agreed upon, made them quiet; I was simply slipping into a state of being suspended in and insulated from the normally felt exigencies of time and place. From deep within me, as if from a separate being, came foreign sounds: groans, whimpers, whining, a low cry that gradually mounted to a full wail. I shook with someone's sobs until aware, still in an entranced, dreamlike way, that these were mine and that I was racked with apparent grief. The anonymous hands continued to slide slowly, to pulse, to knead and prod and cup and caress with uncommon knowledge, familiar yet with an innocent purpose, until my crying abated. Then the hands moved lightly, patting, smoothing, tickling in airy patterns of circles barely brushing the uplifted hairs on the backs of my arms and legs, and I sank into sleep as one drugged by opium.

I cannot say how long I slept. Assad said it was only a few minutes, although it felt like the hundred years of an enchanted sleeping princess. When I awoke, an attendant draped me in a soft white towel, the plushest and most luxurious I had ever felt upon my skin, and led me to the bathing room. There I saw my—as what should I refer to him? My captor? Owner? Companion of the road?

Since agreeing to accompany him to his home in Daghestan, demanding (and receiving) the same amount of money he paid, I felt that Assad regarded me in a new, somewhat confusing light. I think he must have expected me to fight him, and my willingness to go along with him toward the mysterious, ominous East, place of rebirth and disaster, left him puzzled as to the nature of Western womanhood.

And what about poor, devious, misguided Sergei? For now I have only pity for the errant Russian and wonder with genuine interest about his fate: did he return to Batumi to a tired wife and a sullen brood, a life in which his expectations exceeded his means, or did he find another gullible Englishman to tease and hoodwink?

Assad was playing backgammon as he stood in the water at the edge of the pool, the steamy, slightly sulphurous water clouding the air of the room. His opponent, the establishment's owner, rolled a pair of dice out of a rectangular cup and moved two of his stones. His were a yellowed ivory and Assad's ebony. I watched them from a distance, content to loll and soak, feeling the grime of the road washed from my pores. I had been cleansed with soap while asleep, I learned, and rinsed with a warm cloth, and not awakened, so profound had been my slumber. A group of four or five women watched with me, but the rest were intent on their own lively communion in tight loaves and loosely hung clotheslines of female concerns, and it buoyed my spirit to be among them, knowing not a word they spoke and yet feeling akin to each daughter and niece and wife and grandmother as if I belonged to her by blood. The young women who stood giggling as Assad and his friend alternately raised their voices in triumph and protest, depending on the particular move—a block, a capture, a narrow escape through the slightest of gaps—it became clear were those of the assembled most ready for marriage.

Their breasts were high and firm. Nowhere on their bodies could I see the effects of childbirth or child-rearing; their skin would have glowed, unblemished, with or without the steam and the oil. I looked down at my own pallor, the pouches of slack skin, the moles, the cant of uneven breasts, and knew in an instant what it must have been for Adam and for Eve when first they were made aware of their nakedness. Surely it was not the mere fact of their being uncovered before the eyes of God that made them hide, but the awareness of their inadequacy, for they were not as naturally sleek as the great languid cat stretched above their heads upon a limb of the Tree of Life, nor as uniformly clad in fur, nor as symmetrical in three dimensions as a fish, nor as armoured as the thickly mailed rhinoceros. In the presence of these ripe maidens, who were so openly sensual, I wanted to cover myself and to pull my man—it startled me to say it in that way; that I could envision being so quickly and completely owner of and owned by another!—away from the adoring, inviting, long-lashed, simmering dark eyes of his audience.

How terrible, like the shock of ice water when one is expecting the soupy balm of a bath, to be made in an instant undone by doubt. And to find oneself caring that a thing go one way or another, when mere hours before that thing had no presence in one's consciousness. I was uncomfortably aware of my foreignness, my dependence upon Assad. For all my earlier yearning for the unknown, the dangerous and the unexpected, had I been able to will my body back to Henry and Reginald's safe carriage, I think I would.

Oh, I thought, *give me a week's worth of Higgins-tagged documentation to sort through, a month of stale sandwich lunches at my desk, a year of arctic Ottawa winters and another of ankle-swelling, mosquito-infested summers!*

Home. The stifling scrutiny of Mrs. Maxwell's boarding house. The dry, dusty dreariness of Sunday afternoon tea in her threadbare parlour. The pretentiousness of society in the nation's capital, a club I aspired to vaguely but knew I would never join, either by choice or circumstance. Until now.

Please, I thought, crossing my arms to cover my nakedness, *let me close my eyes, and when they are again open let them see the mighty Ottawa, choked with a plain of bare logs, or the canal, bustling with barge traffic and beside it an endless line of sooty rail cars, or the little white church in Eastview, that most of all—let me awaken to that sight and I will never hearken after heathen adventure again. No,* I promised, *I will devote myself to God and the Virgin Mother and Jesus, perhaps join an order of nuns, marry myself to Christ and travel only from prayer to prayer in my penance and my humble gratitude.*

From Tiflis we took the train to Baku, an ugly place of unfettered industry, the muddy landscape dotted with tall wooden oil derricks, pyramidal in shape. From there it was a five-day journey by carriage north along the shores of the Caspian toward Assad's home in the mountains of Daghestan. The people of his homeland were unique in the world. To outsiders they seemed wild, but such was merely their exuberance, their passion for life.

"There are many rules, as you will see," he said. "You must pay attention. It is difficult to make your way without making mistakes."

He said that when God created Earth it was flat and level like the surface of a calm sea. Thinking to give some graceful relief to every land, the Almighty began to distribute hills and small mountains from a sack. But the Devil did not wish mankind to be granted this gift, and as Allah hovered over the land lying between the Caspian and the Black Seas, the Evil One slipped up beside his sack, slit open the cloth, and all the mountains fell into the plain between the two seas.

As punishment, the Devil was forever barred from the mountainous land created there. Life among the crags would be hard enough without the Master of Troubles.

Assad said that if I abided by three guiding principles, the community would accept me. The first was to show respect for old people, for in their wisdom is the way to God. The second was to submit completely to the customs of the district. Finally I was to remember that money had no value in the mountains; what I said and did would be my only currency. While Shamyl was fighting his war of rebellion against the Russians, the legendary leader amassed a fortune in gold with which he purchased guns, bullets, and explosives. When he knew that after decades of evading the tsar's reach he would be captured, he ordered the gold to be dumped into the Lake of Esan, sacred to all who lived in the mountains. He knew that none of his people would lust for the wealth, since it meant less to them than did the dung of their sheep, and that they would prevent any stranger from defiling the waters of the lake. The location of the treasure, like the location of King Solomon's mines, also believed to be somewhere in these same fabled ranges, was safe forever.

As we passed through innumerable villages dotting the route north from the massive Derbent gate, following the shore of the Caspian, we were met with hard stares and derisive laughter. When I asked Assad why they laughed so, he said that I should not take it as a personal affront. It was simply their way of expressing their surprise at and interest in the way I was dressed. I learned to dress humbly, not showing any jewellery, and to keep my head and face covered.

"The lowest beggar will turn his back on one riding through his village arrayed in his finery," Assad said. Most of the men we saw wore black, their only adornment a simple gold dagger.

Assad had been away from his home for many years, having worked as an independent trader, importing and exporting goods from around the world. He had made the markets of the great cities his home and had seen much of Europe and America. This was his first visit back to his home since the day his father took him by train to Moscow when Assad was fourteen.

"He wished me good luck, handed me a few kopecks, and told me I should find myself a job and a place to live. I didn't know a word of Russian!"

"Will your family be expecting you to be married?"

"Yes, it is expected."

"It was a lucky thing you found me then. And at the right price."

His countenance darkened. "I have been very busy. I was not able to meet...suitable women."

"I'm curious. What makes me suitable?"

"This is not a topic I am comfortable discussing," he said, dismissing my question with a turn of the head.

"I'm sorry if I have offended you," I said, expecting to hear nothing more about it, but he turned back from where he had been gazing out the window of the carriage.

"You will see that marriage, where I come from, is not simply a man and a woman choosing each other. It is a complicated process. Everyone is involved. It is not something a man does on his own. I lived alone, in hotels, boarding houses, and rented rooms, while I ran my affairs. I was away from the familiar places and faces of my youth—my nurse, my companions, the whole structure and tradition of my village. In time you will see. We will marry and you will see what it is I am trying to say."

When we arrived in Assad's village, his old nurse, the woman who had raised him like a foster mother, embraced him. His mother had died giving birth to him, and his father had died only a few years after Assad went away to find work. The woman, weeping and trilling with joy, having had no warning of Assad's return, held him, laughing and wailing alternately. She lifted his arm and thrust her nose into his armpit. After sniffing his chest, face, and hair, the woman smiled contentedly and said something he translated as "Thou hast the smell of a man. It is good."

"Baba would suckle me at her breast again if she still had the milk."

We were established in a *saklya*, a small villa with a balcony and a flat roof. Baba and a man named Zhem, the eunuch who guided Assad during his childhood, lived together in Assad's father's house, as was the custom when there are no heirs nearby to claim property.

I was surprised to learn that Assad advanced no claim on the house and associated property; the *saklya* seemed to be ours without any money changing hands, and the servants—the cook and the housekeeper—appeared to come with the house. They saw their claim to tenancy to be a right rather than a privilege, and their carriage and general attitude suggested that if they were not of noble ancestry then they felt they should be. They carried out their duties effectively and without any air of subservience, the result being a sense that they were the ones completely at ease with their station in life, while Assad and I strove to be accommodating.

Baba came each morning to read Assad passages of scripture and to chant incantations in preparation for his marriage. She did not know how to relate to me. According to their tradition, I should have been living in another household until the day of the wedding, and perhaps for months afterward, but housing was at a premium in the village, and new houses could not be built until spring. The place we were given had been vacant only a few days, its occupant, an old *abrek*, having been carried off in his sleep by dreams of glory and bloodshed. The *abrek* had been a wild man in his youth. He fought alongside Shamyl, was wounded many times, and was imprisoned at different occasions by the Russians, Turks, and Lesghians. His family had been embroiled in a blood feud his entire life, and virtually all his male relatives were killed or forced into exile by it. He came to this village as an old man because no one knew him here. The *abrek* had a hidden stash of money, which he lived on discreetly, every day believing he would be dragged from his bed by his enemies, the brothers and sons of those he had killed with his own rifle.

One day a mullah came to minister to us in preparation for the marriage. He was an itinerant scribe and preacher of Islam who spoke only Arabic, and so Baba was brought forward to interpret his words. It was such an event that the entire village of 250 people seemed gathered inside the tiny house, the overflow spilling outside, listening at the doors and open windows. The mullah came to this region only a few times a year, preaching from the Koran, advising in matters of religion and local politics, helping to settle disputes. Wherever he went he found the one or two people who could speak Arabic. In a mountainous region such as this, where hundreds of languages are spoken and where it is rare and dangerous for people to travel too far from familiar surroundings, the mullah acted as an agent of cohesion, for with the word of Allah and Mohammed he brought the news from far-flung parts, and it was this gossip as much as spiritual guidance that the people craved from him.

The mullah asked many questions about me and was dissatisfied with the answers Baba gave him. Here was Assad's future wife, an unbeliever, a foreigner, a woman with no family and as such far poorer than the poorest pauper in the dirtiest soulless city. None of the customary steps leading to the marriage had been followed. The mullah told Baba it was a mistake for Assad to be entering into this union. I asked her if she had relayed the mullah's sentiment to Assad, and she replied that she had not. Baba regarded me in a way, however, that suggested she still might tell him if I did not watch my step.

In the spring, although I was older than most of them by a decade, I began to go to the well every evening to fetch water with the girls of the village. Doing so served two purposes: it allowed me to experience vicariously the courtship ritual as it progressed from its earliest stirrings (as if I had never been in love!). I was also to act as an unofficial chaperone to the maidens, although I was warned not to interfere with what transpired there. It was customary that the unwed girls went to the well unaccompanied by either eunuchs or older women, but since I was already betrothed and an outsider, I was afforded the special status of limited participant and observer.

Six or seven of us ventured with large earthenware pitchers to the well as the sun hung just above the mountaintops. I felt as if I had done nothing for the long, dark months of winter except sit, mend clothes, try to bend my mind and tongue around the local dialect, and learn the songs my husband would expect me to sing to him each evening. And yet I was as content as I had ever been in my life.

Assad and I occupied separate bedrooms in the house. We took our meals at different times of the day, I with the servants and he alone. In the late afternoon, after resting, we walked together, conversing for an hour or more. I told him about my poet, about our noontime walks to Eastview, Lampman's verse, his passion, and his death. Assad listened, not speaking until I had finished. He asked few questions, but those that he did ask revealed that he had been listening intently and thinking about how my love for Archie had changed me.

At first I refused to believe, as he suggested, that I was not letting myself mourn properly, that I was desperately grasping, holding close to my bosom the selfish need to keep my love intact, unchanged and safe. It was he who first advised that I accompany the young girls to the well and watch one courtship in particular closely, that in my mind I should take the place of the girl and be drawn into the attraction of one heart to another. I should not think about Lampman, he said. I should not even picture Assad there in place of the young man. I should simply be that girl, losing my identity for a spell, and only then would the poison of grief be drawn from me.

The young men gathered each evening not far from the well. They sat in a circle to talk about the subject they were most passionate about: warfare and its spoils. I could tell that was what they were discussing, for all their gestures indicated it: here was one aiming and firing a rifle, here another letting gold, silver, jewels rain through his fingers. Sometimes they all laughed in unison as if someone had told a funny story, and sometimes they bent forward to keep some morsel of intrigue private. It never occurred to me that men could be as agitated a knot of gossips as could women. So intent were they in their tight circle that not even the arrival of the girls, it seemed, was a distraction.

In fact, the men ignored us for days on end. We came, tied our containers by their handles to the well's rope one at a time, and let them descend slowly. I learned to slow my movements, to let the pitcher sink in leisurely fashion to the water, to wait patiently long after the time when one might expect it to be filled, and to haul it up with smooth, unhurried strokes hand over hand. This was a spectacle, after all, but I wondered for whom.

One day I hoisted my jug upon my shoulders and turned toward the circle of men. Ignore me, would they! I made the sound of clearing my throat. We had trudged to the well and back every evening for three weeks and not once did a single pair of male eyes look up to acknowledge our presence. It was insupportable! I was so frustrated I was afraid I would scream. Choose one maiden and watch her closely? Observe the courtship from a close distance? What courtship? Nothing was happening. Every day the same group of oblivious men, squatting, arguing, smoking their pipes, acting out their violent triumphs; every day the little parade of water carriers on exhibition.

I stood with my feet planted wide apart, pitcher full to the brim with cold water sloshing over the lip as I swayed to steady it, and cleared my throat. Hello! Yes, over here. We exist, it was meant to say. In truth I might just as well have shot off a gun over their smug heads, for to a man, a dozen of them, they turned, some jumping to their feet. They regarded me for a moment as one might consider a burning house that is beyond hope of salvage, and then they dispersed without uttering another word.

Many days passed before I returned to the well. It was apparent that during my absence an amorous interest had sparked between one of the girls, Irini, who was my favourite, and a boy named Akmed Ibrahim. To a pair of uninitiated eyes nothing extraordinary had transpired. Unless one knew what to look for, it appeared that the same circumstances that had led to my outburst of frustration were still in effect. The first clue to the change was that when it was Irini's turn to fill her pitcher she did so with an added flourish. She held her chin a degree higher than usual, her shoulders slightly farther back, her pelvis tilted up and forward. She threw back her veil when she hoisted the full container onto her shoulder and kept her eyes trained downward until the instant she was closest to Ibrahim, who sat with his back to the well, and who conspicuously did not contribute to the choir of contentious male voices. The eyes of the men darted to Ibrahim's face, their tongues not stilled in the least, but their glances at him becoming quicker and more numerous as Irini approached. It was as if they were trying to send their thoughts to the boy. How he would suffer mortally in front of his elders to be called "boy" to his face, but in truth he was but a mere babe with not a hair on his face and the smooth, unblemished skin any bride would pay dearly to have.

Irini slowed, Ibrahim turned his head, she looked up but dared not meet his gaze, and he turned away only to miss seeing the corner of her mouth turn up into a cherubic smile. It made my heart clutch and ache to see it. I felt privy to something that was much more than a fleeting scrap of time such as we daily rush through, ignorant of its beauty, toward the next and again the next, not knowing what it is we reach for. All we know is that it is rarely the present upon which we invest all the life savings of our hearts.

That night, for the first time since Archie's death, I failed to think and dream about my own, but instead stayed awake until dawn contemplating the lovers at the well, two who had probably played together as children, and who were now as strange to each other and as necessary as is wood to fire. That instant of unstained inevitability, when his eyes left her cheek and her smile embraced the spot his gaze had warmed, I reproduced over and over the way a child will play with the fragile strands leading to her adulthood. His thoughts, hers, what their first words to each other would be, where upon their bodies they would first touch, at what moment would they first fall into each other's eyes and say, "We are alone and the whole world is in us."

When finally I slept, I dreamed I was standing in the Beechwood Cemetery, a place I had not found the courage to visit, but which in the dream I could picture clearly. Although snow covered the ground to a depth that obscured the writing on two adjacent tombstones, I knew whose they were. I heard two distinct voices, a woman's, crying and pleading, and a man's, rhythmically metered as if he were reading aloud. The voice was deeper, older, more reverberant than I remembered Archie's to have been, but his recitation struck me as being something familiar, one of his longer poems, "City of the End of Things" perhaps, except that upon waking I could not remember a word of it.

Maud's voice continued throughout, sobbing, begging him, not that he should stop and not that she should be let out of her grave, but that she be let into his. Frantically I began to claw at the snow with my bare fingers at a spot between the two headstones. The voices grew louder, as if they knew I knelt above them and they were urging me on, but I could not dig through to the bottom of the snow layer. The deeper I went the more the frozen ground receded. The last thing I remembered before waking was the sense of being wedged into a dark, airless snow hole, its suffocating walls translucent and grey.

In the mountains where I began my second life, the pastures were again blushing green. Each evening Irini and Ibrahim exchanged increasingly bold and more open glances at the village well. One of the boy's older brothers called upon Assad to ask him if he would go to Irini's father to negotiate her *kalym* or price. After the young man left with Assad's assurance that he would he honoured to act as Ibrahim's emissary, I asked him what was meant by "her price."

"Please don't tell me she is to be bought. There is altogether too much buying and selling of female flesh in this society. Why does she not get together a war chest full of treasure and buy him?"

Assad laughed at me in a way that made me even angrier. He tried to explain that in his world a woman was not being bought when she got married, nor was a father enticing prospective suitors with a dowry in order that one of them take his daughter off his hands. Instead, in addition to a gift to her family, the young man pledged his intention to provide for his future wife by offering a sum of money that would be hers alone to control, and which would afford her some semblance of financial independence in the marriage.

Jokingly I asked whether or not he was going to give me such a legacy, but his visage grew dark, and he did not answer, leaving me feeling all the more confused. He said that if the man did not have sufficient wealth to make an offer for the woman he desired to marry, then he had to do one of two things. Either he must go off on a thieving expedition in some distant territory or he must kidnap the girl, fleeing her avenging family and putting himself under the protection of the prince of the land. Like the church that provides sanctuary to all who demand it, the prince is under an obligation of honour to protect the lovers and eventually to argue the young man's case before his love's family, often offering to pay her *kalym* himself.

"I would never debase myself in such a humiliating way before the local prince," Assad said. "I know him. He is a pretender who tricked the Russians into granting him a title. He uses his newfound wealth to control those in his debt."

I tried to convince him that I had no need of such a costly gift. I was strong. I was with him of my own volition. He had nothing to fear from my family. As he had assured, I was free to go whenever I wanted, and he would ensure that I had safe transportation as far as Baku or Sebastopol or Istanbul or London itself. I was living again. As long as I could spend some part of each day in his company, I needed nothing more.

Assad and Ibrahim disappeared for a week with the other able-bodied men of the village. When they returned, I asked him where he had gone and why. He only winked and laughed. It was an expedition and they had returned with great riches. That was all he said and, frankly, all I wanted to know. The important thing in everyone's mind was that now the marriages could take place, Irini's first then mine. In preparation Ibrahim's representatives met Irini's father to negotiate and pay the amount of the *kalym*.

The marriage feast went on for ten days, the whole village with the exception of the bride and her groom in attendance. Ibrahim was sequestered at the home of a friend to fast and indulge in dreams of love. Each night leading to the wedding day Irini came to pass a few hours with him. They pretended to be doing this in complete secrecy, but everyone in the village knew about it and quietly encouraged the meetings so that the lovers would be certain they were not making a mistake by marrying.

On the morning of her wedding day, Irini, heavily veiled, was "abducted" by several armed friends of Ibrahim's and brought to the feast. There, separated by only a thin curtain, they linked their little fingers.

"Are you capable of being the husband of a woman?" the mullah asked Ibrahim.

"Yes," he said in a strong voice, and the old women in the

hall were heard to murmur protective incantations against any spell of impotence directed at him by his enemies.

That night, after the newlyweds had celebrated separately with their friends, Ibrahim began to make his way to his wife's chamber. At every door he was met by a disguised figure who blocked his way and refused to allow passage until the groom had paid him a few gold coins. When he finally did gain entry, the room was riotous with chickens, the corralling and removal of which took many minutes. Then an old woman, one of Irini's relatives, barged in and prostrated herself on the bed, refusing to budge until Ibrahim had paid her, too, from the booty he had brought back with him from Kislar.

Finally he was able to bar the door, and Irini emerged from hiding, although they were hardly alone, for every minute or so a new disturbance would come, a cat thrown in at the window or a demand that Ibrahim appear on the balcony to sing a song, accompanied from below by boisterous musicians. Between interruptions he continued the laborious task of untying the intricate knots of her corset. He could not cut the strings, for that would have been a sign of weakness and lack of control on his part; he knew that the next day all his friends would arrive to inspect the condition of the stays.

The remarkable thing is that while I saw none of this, I felt as if I were there in the room watching, because at every stage a report would come back to the feast. Now he is through the final door, now he has cleared the room, now he has removed the final veil. One old man announced that he could predict the order of events in the bridal chamber to within a minute, he had attended so many weddings, and a pool was drawn up as to the exact time the shooting would begin.

"Shooting, what shooting?" I asked Assad, who was enjoying watching my often horrified reactions to the news of the various obstacles thrown into the path of the newlyweds.

"When the groom has successfully undressed his bride and convinced himself of her virginity, he goes out onto the balcony and fires off his revolver. On his signal every man within earshot does the same. I must warn you," he added, "the shooting may go on all night."

Soon the shots did begin to ring out, as had been predicted, all over the hall and from outside. The men jumped up from their seats to fire round after round into the ceiling, which began to fall in large chunks of plaster. I screamed. We covered our heads with our hands and ran outside.

Assad was laughing at my shrieks as he burst through the door leading outside. It was a great joke. He was turning his head to say something, perhaps to mention how foolish I was to be afraid on this of all nights, this rehearsal of sorts for our own marriage.

Instead of seeing revellers firing at the moon, we were met by a line of mounted Cossacks. The intruders fired their rifles at point-blank range, picking off the men of the village, the old and the young indiscriminately, one by one as they stumbled out of the feast and into the dark. It was retribution for the bloodless sack of Kislar. A few of the soldiers were killed by return fire. The women were untouched. We could only run for cover and wait. The groom, being the first to fire, had been the first to be shot at from below, but had not been hit. One could not say, however, that he and his bride were untouched, for they were related to many of the dead. After it was over, and the cavalrymen had ridden away, we wept all night and all day, and over the next few days we buried the dead, twenty-three men, Assad among them.

I asked Reginald if he ever got to climb Mount Tamischeira and look down from the spot where the Amazon women had watched the Deluge sweep away their brothers and husbands and sons. He confessed that he had not.

"I ask only because I am curious. I think I know what they must have felt. The remarkable thing is that one goes on. A world is obliterated and still the living continues. It fascinates me. There is no reason for such tenacity. Archibald used to say that our intellect would take us only partway. Do you believe that, Mr. Norman?"

He said that he did not know what he believed, but that he would study the question. We agreed that when we returned home we would each study the question from our peculiar points of view, from opposite sides of the new Atlantic Ocean, and occasionally, when we felt the need, report our findings to the other. We would have to create our own navigation markers, our own Pillars of Hercules, as it were, to guide us in our enquiry. We would have to be prepared to lose them from time to time.

He stumbled over some banal words of consolation and regret. I stopped him.

"I'm not afraid, Henry. You mustn't be, either."

Epilogue

Sometimes I think that the world is too vast. It too quickly swallows the brave and the good, the timid and the dull, leaving no trace. Travel accounts such as mine are being pushed aside by weightier histories, pithier political analyses. I foresee a day when world travellers will carry pocket-sized reference guides to foreign lands, tiny compendia of facts at their fingertips, making the narratives I write obsolete. Perhaps I should anticipate the inevitable and write the first in the series. *The Norman Guide to Erebus*. It would have to be revised every few years. It would be something to fall back on. I will not be an Honourable "Mumbler" forever.

I do not think fear ever entered my thoughts until Katherine mentioned it that day, but now I see that fear was always there. I will always travel, but never so blithely or blindly again. The Far East next, I think. China again? Yes, the inscrutable empire, not a place for the solitary wanderer. I am ready, at last, for a companion.

Acknowledgements

I gratefully acknowledge the financial support of the Canada Council for the Arts and the Nova Scotia Department of Tourism and Culture, which helped me write this book. I also extend a thank-you to Don Domanski for giving me permission to use an excerpt from his poem "Walking Down to Acheron" as an epigraph. The poem originally appeared in the Winter 2002 issue (number 214) of *The Fiddlehead*.

This is a work of fiction. Nothing in the historical record suggests that Reginald Fessenden, Katherine Waddell, and Henry Norman ever met, let alone travelled anywhere together. Furthermore, there is no proof that Miss Waddell and Archibald Lampman were lovers. While I have drawn aspects of my characters from descriptions of the real people, this story is meant to be nothing more than a flight of the imagination.

Fessenden published his theories concerning the Great Flood and the origin of the myth lands in *The Deluged Civilization of the Caucasus Isthmus* (Boston: T. J. Russell, printer, 1923). Special thanks to Sharon Murphy and Christine Hatton at Dalhousie University's Sexton Library of Engineering and Design for finding this rare treatise for me.

Lampman's love for Katherine is suggested by Margaret Coulby Whitridge in her book, *Lampman's Kate* (Ottawa: Borealis Press, 1975), and in her introduction to *The Poems of Archibald Lampman* (Toronto: University of Toronto Press, 1974). Some of Lampman's fictional letters are adapted from those found in *Archibald Lampman: Selected Prose,* Barrie Davies, ed. (Ottawa: The Techumseh Press, 1975).

Henry Norman's book, *All the Russias* (London: William Heinemann, 1902), was an invaluable source of information about the Dariel Pass, Tiflis, and the oil fields of Baku. The quoted passage from Mikhail Lermontov's "The Demon" (Storr, translator) is taken from Norman's book. Of great help also was Chapter 6 ("Baku and Tbilisi") of Laurens Van Der Post's *Journey into Russia* (London: Reprint Society, 1965). I learned about life in Islamic Daghestan from *Twelve Secrets of the Caucasus* (New York: The Viking Press, 1931) by Mohammed Essad-Bey. Sergei Borshelnikov's ragged recitation of Aleksandr Pushkin is based on the Russian poet's own 1835 *Journey to Arzun*, translated by Birgitta Ingemanson (Ann Arbor: Ardis, 1974). Ormand Raby's account of the boyhood friendship of Fessenden and Lampman at Port Hope's Trinity College School, in *Radio's First Voice* (Toronto: Ryerson Press, 1970), gave me the idea of imagining a continuing correspondence between the scientist and the poet.

RICHARD CUMYN was born in Ottawa and has degrees in English and education from Queen's University in Kingston, Ontario. He is the fiction editor for *The Antigonish Review* and has published four collections of short fiction: *The Limit of Delta Y over Delta X* (Goose Lane), *I Am Not Most Places* (Beach Holme), *Viking Brides* (Oberon), and *The Obstacle Course* (Oberon). *Viking Brides* was shortlisted for a ReLit Award in 2002. Cumyn's short stories have appeared in many Canadian literary publications, including *The Journey Prize Anthology*. He lives in Halifax, Nova Scotia.

MORE NEW FICTION

The Moor Is Dark Beneath the Moon
by David Watmough
NOVEL $18.95 CDN $14.95 US ISBN: 0-88878-434-1

After decades in Canada, Davey Bryant returns to Cornwall, England, for the funeral of a mysterious relative and lands in the middle of a property-inheritance squabble that threatens to escalate into something far worse.

Distraught by the changed landscape of his beloved homeland, Davey wanders the lonely moors and is soon sleuthing his way through a farce of megalithic proportions.

Cold Clear Morning
by Lesley Choyce
NOVEL $18.95 CDN $14.95 US ISBN: 0-88878-416-3

Taylor Colby and his childhood sweetheart, Laura, abandoned their Nova Scotia coastal village home for a life in the high-octane world of rock music in California. Now, after Laura's drug-related death, Taylor has returned to his roots to live once again with his noble but isolated boat-builder father. Complicating matters further, Taylor's mother, who has been battling cancer, attempts to reconcile with both her husband and son whom she deserted decades earlier.

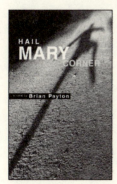

Hail Mary Corner
by Brian Payton
NOVEL $18.95 CDN ISBN: 0-88878-422-8

High on a cliff overlooking a pulp-mill town in British Columbia, sixteen-year-old Bill MacAvoy and his friends lead cloistered lives when other boys their age run free. It may be the fall of 1982, but inside the walls of their Benedictine seminary they inhabit a medieval society steeped in ritual and discipline—a world where black-robed monks move like shadows between doubt and faith.

BEACH HOLME PUBLISHING • WWW.BEACHHOLME.BC.CA